A One-Act Farce
by Casey Bell

Who Shot the Sherriff

Copyright ©2013 Casey Bell

All rights reserved. No part of this publication may be reproduced, stored in a retrieval system or transmitted in any form or by any means, electronic, mechanical, photocopying, recording or otherwise, without the prior written permission of the publisher.

Any production of either of these plays without legal permission may result in a lawsuit. To produced one or both of these plays contact ReadyWriter Co at readywritercsb.com or casey@caseysamuelbell.com or PO Box 5231, Old Bridge, NJ 08857

Published by: BookCase Publishing

ISBN: 9798395952882

Cover Design by Casey Bell

Printed in the United States

Casey Bell
PO Box 5231
Old Bridge, NJ 08857
caseysamuelbell.com
authorcaseybell.com
readywritercsb.com

WHO SHOT THE SHERIFF? A ONE ACT PLAY©

By: Casey Bell

Technical Requirements:

The entire play takes place in the living room of a very wealthy family. There are 5 doors that the actors enter and exit and one doorway (downstairs) and at least one upstairs).

CHARACTERS

COOK: 30 something year old female from the streets. Ebonics is her first language. She used to be a gang member, but fixed up her act, but still has the attitude.

BUTLER: 50 something year old male. Very distinctive, speaks great English. Just by his speech you can tell he is greatly educated. Grew up with Sheriff. (May speak in British accent. But make sure your words are clear).

MAID: 40 something year old female. From the deep south. And has the accent to prove it. She is Sheriff's love child.

NURSE: 20 something year old female. Wears revealing nurse's outfits unconsciously. Used to be a stripper.

GARDENER: 30 something year old Hispanic male. Speaks with Spanish accent.

POOL BOY: 18-year-old Surfer dude who parties more than he works.

WIFE: 40 something year old wealthy female. Sheriff's daughter-in-law.

COP: Any age, gender, ethnicity

E.M.T.: Any age, gender, ethnicity

DETECTIVE: 50 something year old male. Not that bright, but bright enough to solve the case.

BABY GIRL: 9-year-old female. She is Little Red Riding Hood on the outside but the wolf on the inside.

WHO SHOT THE SHERIFF?
ACT ONE SCENE ONE

This play takes place within a day. The scene opens empty. There is no one on stage just a set. This play takes place entirely in WIFE*'s living room. It's the home of a wealthy family. (Set designer be creative). The play begins with a silent stage. Within minutes (or seconds) a gunshot is heard then a scream.*

COOK

(Enters; frightened she looks around to see what happened. Soon BUTLER enters).

Yo, what the hell was that?

BUTLER

It sounded like a gun shot.

COOK

Hell naw! Not in da house.

BUTLER

I am unaware. Are you okay?

COOK

Yeah, just tryin' ta figga out what's going on.

BUTLER

Were you the one who screamed?

COOK

Naw. Should we call the po-po?

BUTLER

I do not know…I am unaware of the actions we should take. We are unaware of what is taking place.

MAID

(Enters). Lawd, have mercy! Did ya'll hear that? It sounded like a gun.

BUTLER

Were you the one who screamed?

MAID

Yeah-yes.

COOK

Whatcha screaming fo? Did your ass get shot?

MAID

No.

BUTLER

Then why would you produce such an ear-piercing noise?

MAID

It was a good sound effect. Are ya'll okay?

COOK

We fine. How you doin'?

MAID

I'm fine. I was just in the bathroom over yonder. I wuz cleaning like I'supposed to and *"Bang!"* I jumped and spilled bleach all over the place. It smells like crazy in there.

COOK

I can imagine.

BUTLER

Did you open the windows?

MAID

Yeah, but it'll take a mighty long time before that strong smells go away. Whatch ya'll think happened

COOK

We don't know.

MAID

Should we phone the police?

BUTLER

We don't know.

MAID

Well, then what shall we do?

COOK AND BUTLER

We don't know!

NURSE

(Enters) Oh my goodness, oh my goodness! Was that like a gun shot? Because if it was that would totally be as if.

BUTLER

I believe it was.

NURSE

Well, who is like shooting guns like in here?

COOK

We don't know a damn thing.

NURSE

This is like totally far out. Is everyone like totally, okay?

COOK

I'm fine.

BUTLER

I am a bit startled.

MAID

I'm bleached.

NURSE

Oh, this totally can't be good. I am totally too pretty to die.

COOK

What makes you think you gonna die?

NURSE

Because if the murderer is still like in the house he might totally come after us.

MAID

Well, what makes you thank there's a murderer in the house. It was just a shot. And we don't even know if it was from a gun.

NURSE

Da, where else would a gun shot like come from?

BUTLER

It could have been fireworks or even a car back firing.

GARDENER

(Enters) What is goin' on? Whatch you doin'?

COOK

Yo, we just chatting it up 'bout the gunshot we just heard.

GARDNER

Whatcha ya doin' just standin' around? We should do sumting.

MAID

What weze supposed ta do?

GARDNER

I zon't know, call thee cops.

COOK

What the hell we tell 'em? We don't know what's up.

GARDNER

Just szay you hear a gun.

BUTLER

But what if it was not a gun shot.

MAID

Like maybe it was totally Sheriff just practicing or something.

GARDENER

Well where iz he? Where iz Sheriff?

BUTLER

I am under the impression that no one has the knowledge of his location.

GARDENER

Well, someone should see if he's okay.

COOK

Yo, I'm not going up there, I can get shot.

MAID

Well, I's can't go. Butler, I thank you should go on up dem stairs and see that Sherriff is alright.

BUTLER

What? That is a despicable idea. I will not stand the chance of getting shot.

NURSE

Well, I totally cannot go. Besides, Gardner it was like totally your idea, so you should go.

GARDENER

I no go up dem stairs.

COOK

Yo, we gots ta figga out who gonna be going up dem stairs.

BUTLER

And how are we going to make that decision?

GARDENER

Well, let's takey vote. On zee count of tree we will all say someone else's name. The name that is heard thee most will go.

COOK

That sounds fair.

GARDENER

Okay on zee count of tree. One, tu, tree…

POOL BOY

(Enters). Yo dudes did you hear that?

COOK, GARDENER, BUTLER, MAID, and NURSE

POOL BOY!

POOL BOY

Yeah?

COOK

Yo, you won the vote, man. You gotta get up dem stairs and see what's up.

POOL BOY

Yo, what vote? Whatcha ya talking about?

NURSE

Like didn't you totally hear the gun shot?

POOL BOY

Yeah, dude, but what vote?

GARDENER

Someone hastee go up the stairs and see what's going on. We voted djew, which means, djew have to go up zee stairs and see who shot twho.

POOL BOY

Yo, this is totally bonkers. I didn't even know you dudes were voting.

WIFE

(Enters with shopping bags) Oh, my goodness. That is the last time I go shopping on a Monday morning. That place was full of people. You would think everyone would be at work. *(Short pause, frustrated)*. What's going on? Why is everyone just sitting around? Shouldn't you all be laboring hard at work?

NURSE

We're totally not sitting, we're standing.

WIFE

Sitting standing it doesn't matter. You're supposed to be working. I pay for you to work. What is going on? What are you doing, having a social party?

COOK

Wife. Child, I got some bad news for you.

WIFE

What? Oh no, they took Susan Lucci's Emmy away from her. Why!? And after 19 nominations. They are so unfair.

COOK

No, girl. It's much worse than that

WIFE

Well, then what is it?

COOK

Yo, someone got shot.

WIFE

Shot? What do you mean shot? Who?

BUTLER

We do not have any solid information at the moment. All we know is that a sound that familiars a gun shot was heard in the upper section of the house.

WIFE

Well, what are you doing standing around? Go upstairs and see what's going on.

NURSE

Are you like totally crazy? What if the shooter is totally still in the house? He may just try to shoot us, like totally.

WIFE

Well, where is Sheriff?

GARDENER

No one knows, signora.

WIFE

(To the audience) Do you know where the Sheriff is? *(Frustrated)* My goodness. Must I do everything in this house? *(She walks upstairs and she opens the door to Sheriff's room, she enters then screams, she exits).* Someone shot Sheriff. Dial 9-1-1.

BUTLER

(Dials the phone). Yes, this is an emergency. Someone has shot the Sheriff. Please arrive immediately.

MAID

(Sirens are heard. COP enters) Well, what took ya'll so long?

COP

(Enters) Okay everybody freeze. *(Everybody freezes).* Okay somebody start talking. Who shot the Sheriff? Okay someone needs to talk. Stop playing around, start talking. Who the hell shot the Sheriff? Okay, damn it, everyone unfreeze. *(Everyone unfreezes)* Now start talking.

MAID

We don't know a thang, officer. We just heard the shot, but didn't see a thang.

COP

(An E.M.T. enters, he runs upstairs). Okay, by the time that guy returns with the Sheriff, someone had better told me something.

BUTLER

Cop, we seriously do not have any substantial information.

WIFE

(The E.M.T. returns, he runs down stairs and exit with a dummy). Nooooo! Why?! Who did it? Which one of you ingrates shot my father?

MAID

In law, your father-in-law.

COP

Okay, somebody better start talking.

Simultaneously

BUTLER: After hearing the shot I came to see what had transpired.

MAID: I wha-en't even upstairs when I heard the shot.

GARDENER: I was outside planting in dee garden.

NURSE: I was totally in the study when I heard the bang.

WIFE: I was at the supermarket.

POOL BOY: Yo, dude, I was cleaning the pool.

COOK: I was cooking.

COP

Okay, one at a time.

WIFE

This is hopeless. Shouldn't you be upstairs searching for clues? Apparently one of Sheriff's workers shot him.

COOK

Yo, how we know you ain't shoot 'em?

WIFE

Why would I shoot my own father?

MAID

In law, your father-in-law.

WIFE

I was at the supermarket.

COOK

So, you say. Who's ta say you weren't here the whole time?

WIFE

Did you not see me come in with the bags?

MAID

You could have stuffed those bags with things from the cooler.

WIFE

How? Cook was in the kitchen the whole time.

BUTLER

And how would you know that information?

WIFE

She's the cook. Where else would she be?

MAID

You could have prepared those bags last night knowin' you was gonna shoot 'em.

WIFE

This is ridiculous. Cop, are you going to arrest them and take them all in?

COP

No.

WIFE

Then what are you going to do?

COP

I am going to make way for…Detective.

NURSE

Like who?

COP

Detective.

POOL BOY

Dude, who's that?

DETECTIVE

(Enters). That is me.

GARDENER

Who is me?

DETECTIVE

Detective. Sly Detective. I like my drinks stirred, not shaken, my ladies rough and my cases…hot. For I am Sly Detective and I will solve this case. Now tell me, who shot the Sheriff?

COOK

No one knows, Detective. That's why you're here.

DETECTIVE

If that's the case then that means it time to figure out…Who Shot The Sheriff?

(Blackout).

ACT ONE SCENE TWO

The scene opens with WIFE, MAID, COOK, NURSE, POOL BOY, BUTLER, and GARDENER sitting waiting patiently. Within minutes DETECTIVE enters.

DETECTIVE

So, I have evaluated the scene and came to a conclusion.

MAID

What?

DETECTIVE

Well, there was a bullet cap on the floor next to Sheriff's bed, there is also a bullet hole in the wall next to his bed, last, but not least, there is a gun that has been fired on the floor. I have come to the conclusion that someone has shot the Sheriff.

COOK

(Sarcastically) Wow. You figga-ed that out all by yo-self?

WIFE

By the way, have you heard from the doctor? How is my father-in-law doing?

DETECTIVE

He is doing just fine. He is unconscious at the moment, but he is breathing. He was shot in the ear.

MAID

In the ear?

DETECTIVE

Much blood was lost, but they think they can save him.

WIFE

Oh my word, that is horrible. Is there anything we can do for him?

DETECTIVE

No, but next time don't wait so long to call the police.

WIFE

This is just horrific. Detective, you have to hurry up and find out who shot the Sheriff. Were there any clues in the room? Were there any finger prints on the gun?

DETECTIVE

No. There were none. Which means the shooter was wearing gloves.

WIFE

Then that could have been anyone of you. You all wear gloves while you're working.

COOK

You wear gloves too.

WIFE

I didn't shoot my father.

MAID

In law, your father-in-law.

WIFE

Why do you keep implying that I shot him?

MAID

What makes ya thank I implied ya shot 'em? Is your conscience feelin' guilty?

WIFE

My conscience is innocent, but you keep implying that I shot my father.

MAID

In law, your father-in-law.

WIFE

See, there you go again. Why do you keep mentioning that he's an in-law? As if because he's an in-law and not my real father, I would shoot him.

MAID

I'm not implying anythang.

WIFE

You implied that and you know it.

MAID

I didn't imply anythang.

DETECTIVE

Whoever denied it implied it. Okay that's enough of that. What we have to figure out is after the shooting, who came in from outside.

MAID

Wife, came in from the outside.

BUTLER

So did Gardener and Pool Boy.

DETECTIVE

Then that means one of you shot him.

GARDENER

What do djew mean?

DETECTIVE

In Sheriff's room, the window was opened and the screen was missing. Which means either the shooter entered the room from the window or made his or her escape from the window.

WIFE

Well, which one of you made *his* escape through the window?

POOL BOY

Yo, brah, I'm petrified of heights.

GARDENER

I told you I was in the garden, signor. Besides I don't know how to use a gun.

COOK

You wouldn't have to. Whoever shot him had bad aim.

GARDENER

How do we know it wasn't you?

COOK

Oh, please, if I was gonna shoot him I woulda shot 'em dead in the ass.

WIFE

Detective, I think you should go back upstairs and find more evidence.

DETECTIVE

Please, don't tell me how to do my job.

POOL BOY

Dude, I agree with Wife. You need to find more evidence so you can figure out that I didn't do it, brah.

GARDENER

I no shoot 'em either.

WIFE

And neither did I.

BUTLER

We are not getting any closer to solving the issue.

WIFE

Butler is right. Detective you have to hurry up and find out who shot my daddy.

MAID

In law, your daddy-in-law.

COOK

Can we hurry this up, I gotta finish cooking.

DETECTIVE

No one is going anywhere. Not until I figure out which one of you shot the Sheriff.

COOK

But that can take foreva. You already doin' a bad job.

DETECTIVE

I don't care. I know one of you shot him which means one of you is lying. Now everyone just sit quietly. I am about to interrogate you so the audience knows your motives.

BABY GIRL

(Enters skipping. She is wearing scarf and gloves). Hi mommy.

WIFE

Hey Baby Girl, how are you?

DETECTIVE

And who is this?

COOK

That's Baby Gurl. Wife's and Husband's daughter.

DETECTIVE

How did she get in the house? The door was locked.

WIFE

She lives here, Detective. She has a key.

BABY GIRL

Mommy, who is this strange man?

WIFE

This is Detective. He's here to figure out which one of these workers shot your grandpa.

BABY GIRL

(Gasps) Oh, no. Gramps was shot?

WIFE

Yes he was.

BABY GIRL

He's dead, right? I mean he's not going to die is he? I just couldn't survive without him.

DETECTIVE

No, he's fine Little Girl.

BABY GIRL

The name is Baby Girl.

DETECTIVE

Oh, sorry. Baby Girl. *(Beat)* Baby Girl, where were you today around 1PM.

BABY GIRL

I was in school Detective.

WIFE

Wait a second. What are you implying?

DETECTIVE

I am simply doing my job.

WIFE

You don't actually think Baby Girl shot the Sheriff? She's Baby Girl; she doesn't know how to use a gun.

COOK

Again, just to remind everyone, the shooter had bad aim.

WIFE

And what are you implying?

GARDENER

You must stop accusing people of implying things.

WIFE

And what are you implying by that?

DETECTIVE

Okay, that's enough. From now on during the rest of this play you cannot use the word imply in any form. Now Baby Girl are you sure you were in school?

BABY GIRL

Of course.

DETECTIVE

Baby Girl, if you were in school then tell me what you learned.

BABY GIRL

I learned many things in all of my classes. Which class do you want me to talk about?

DETECTIVE

What did you learn in Algebra?

WIFE

For goodness sake Detective, she's a nine year old girl. She's not in Algebra yet.

BABY GIRL

Mommy, what's Algebra?

WIFE

It's annoying. *(Beat)* Look this is getting ridiculous.

COOK

It's been ridiculous.

WIFE

Detective, would you please just hurry this up. You're wasting time questioning Baby Girl. She was in school when Pool Boy or Gardener shot him.

POOL BOY AND GARDENER

Hey.

COOK

I really need ta get back ta the kitchen and finish cookin'. When is you gonna 'rest somebody?

DETECTIVE

When I figure out which one of you shot him.

COOK

Well, could we at least take a break?

BUTLER

Yes, please, this is becoming strenuous.

DETECTIVE

Fine. We will take a short break. Lights please *(Blackout)*.

ACT ONE SCENE THREE

The scene is a continuation of the prior scene nothing changes. When the lights come up everyone continues.

MAID

Well, that was a nice break.

POOL BOY

Dude it was short.

DETECTIVE

You know what, why don't you guys watch TV? Relax enjoy the nice fresh homely air. I am going to go upstairs and do some more research in Sheriff's room. And absolutely no one is allowed to leave this room. Understand? *(All agree with adlib. BABY GIRL turns on the television. Everyone sits and relaxes. Detective talks to himself)* Before I go upstairs I think I will interrogate someone. Who should I pick? *(DETECTIVE thinks for a bit).*

MAID

(To Butler). You wanna help me clean the bleach up off the floor in the bathroom over yonder?

BUTLER

Sure. *(MAID and BUTLER exit to bathroom).*

DETECTIVE

(He approaches COOK. COOK is reading a book, the cover reads, "How To Shoot People in the Ear"). Hi, Cook. How are you?

COOK

Yo, just chillin' And how you doin'?

DETECTIVE

A little backed up. I had too much cheese on my omelet this morning. But other than that I'm fine. *(Beat)* So, Cook. Tell me about yourself.

COOK

Is you flirtin' wit me?

DETECTIVE

No. I just want some information. To see if you have a motive to shoot Sheriff.

COOK

I love Sheriff. Besides, I shot him once before. And I made a vow that I would never shoot him again. And I don't break my vows.

DETECTIVE

Why did you shoot him?

COOK

Because I needed a job. I told 'em if he didn't get me a job I would shoot 'em. I shot 'em, he gave me the job, end of story. Besides Wife shot him.

DETECTIVE

Why would she shoot her father? Well, her in-law, father-in-law.

COOK

That's just the thing. She tryin' ta act like she love 'em and everythang, but she begged Husband to move 'em into a nursing home. She kept sayin' she didn't wanna take care of his ass. That's why Husband hired Nurse. But Wife was against it from the start.

DETECTIVE

That's some vital information. Thank you Cook.

COOK

Uh um.

DETECTIVE

(Looks over towards WIFE and walks towards her. He sits next to her. WIFE is holding a newspaper (or magazine) up to her face; it reads "I Didn't Do It.") Hey, Wife, may I talk to you? *(WIFE nods yes).* Do you really love Sheriff as your father?

WIFE

He's like a second father to me and I love him. He is such a great man. He was one of those parents that said I am not losing a son, but gaining a daughter. Sherriff went to a father daughter dance with me *(Reminiscing, still angry)* that my real father could not attend because he was too busy for his own daughter. Can you believe that too busy to accompany his own flesh and blood to a dance? *(Attacking DETECTIVE)* Is that fair daddy?!

DETECTIVE

(Everyone reacts by looking in confusion) Girl, calm down, I'm not your father.

WIFE

(Collecting herself). Sorry. Either or I owe Sheriff a lot for making me feel special that day. So, you see I just could not shoot him. But Gardener, however.

DETECTIVE

Why do you think that?

WIFE

Well, I overheard a conversation him and Sheriff was having a few days ago. I was afraid something like this would happen, but I didn't know what to do. You see, Gardener has been working for Sheriff for years, decades. He was one of the staff members that moved here with Sheriff when he fell ill. Maid, Cook, and Gardener were all his staff at his home. Well, anyways, Gardener asked him for a raise and Sheriff told him no. And then Sheriff reminded him that he was an illegal alien and could have him shipped back if he didn't watch his tone. Then they started arguing and then the last thing

Sheriff said was only over my dead body. And Gardener said, then so be it, watch your back.

DETECTIVE

Wow.

WIFE

I know, isn't that amazing. When you said that either Pool Boy or Gardener shot him I knew it was Gardener

DETECTIVE

I also said you could have shot him.

WIFE

I did not shoot my father-in-law.

DETECTIVE

Well, thank you for talking to me.

WIFE

Any time Detective. You just better find out who did it.

DETECTIVE

Oh, I will.

WIFE

How do you know?

DETECTIVE

Because I read the end of the play. *(MAID and BUTLER enters in all white garments (including shoes) looking amazed at what the bleach did to their clothing. COOK looks at them in confusion and they return the look as if nothing happened. DETECTIVE approaches GARDENER. NURSE exits to study).* May I speak with you for a moment?

GARDENER

Si, signor?

DETECTIVE

Grace-e-us. So, Gardener, what do you do for Sheriff?

GARDENER

I plant and harvest all of his food. I pretty much grow everything Cook cooks.

DETECTIVE

Do you grow the meat? *(He laughs. GARDENER looks confused. SHERIFF giggles)* It was a joke. *(No response).* Never mind. So, Gardener, how much do you like Sheriff?

GARDENER

Oh, I really like him. He done a lot per me and me Madre. You know he paid per me Madre's surgery.

DETECTIVE

What kind of surgery?

GARDENER

Me Madre's boobs were lop-sided. He paid for her to have a surgery to make them even. I could never shoot such a generous hombre. *(Whispering)* Besides, I have a feeling Nurse shot him.

DETECTIVE

Really, why?

GARDENER

Well, it all starts back when he first got sick and Husband had to hire Nurse. When Sheriff met Nurse, he realized she was dee stripper he met down at dee club.

DETECTIVE

Nurse is a stripper? And she dresses so humbly.

GARDENER

Well, Sheriff still requests lap dances. But she refuses and every time she does Sheriff tells her He is going to tell Governor that she used to be a stripper. Governor is her father and he would be devastated if he found out his lola was a stripper. I think she shot him to put an end to the lap dances.

DETECTIVE

Wow, this is just amazing. This house is just full of psychos. Thanks for the information.

GARDENER

No problemo, signor.

DETECTIVE

(NURSE enters with wine bottle and wine glass. She pours herself a glass of wine and then drinks from the wine bottle. DETECTIVE approaches NURSE. WIFE exits to room). Hey, may I speak to you. *(She nods yes and takes another sip from the bottle).* So, how are you doing?

NURSE

I'm totally as if about this shooting thing. I just totally hope it will like end soon.

DETECTIVE

Oh, it won't be soon. We have a couple of more scenes to go through. So, why should I believe you didn't shoot him?

NURSE

I could totally never shoot anyone. And you know why? Because I am a Johnson and we Johnson's totally don't go around shooting people. Besides, I kinda knew this would totally happen. I knew Butler could not work here any longer without doing something to Sheriff.

DETECTIVE

Butler? Why Butler?

NURSE

Well, Butler and Sheriff are really totally old friends. They grew up together. But, they separated because Sheriff totally stole Butler's girlfriend.

DETECTIVE

Secretary was Butler's girlfriend?

NURSE

Yes. And Secretary is her middle name. Her first name is Administrative. Anyway, Sheriff and Administrative eloped and when they returned Butler and Sheriff had this totally drama-gantic argument and vowed never to see each other again. Husband had no clue about this when he hired Butler, and Butler didn't even realize that Husband was Sheriff's son. When Sheriff got the sniffles and moved in that's when Butler and Sheriff reunited. And the tension in here ever since has been like, oh my gosh.

DETECTIVE

This is interesting information. Thank you.

NURSE

Like totally.

DETECTIVE

(WIFE *enters with a shirt that reads: "I Love My Father-in-Law." She sits back down and reads her newspaper (or magazine).* BABY GIRL *exits to kitchen.* POOL BOY *exits to backyard (pool)* DETECTIVE *walks towards* BUTLER). Hey Butler, may I talk to you?

BUTLER

And what shall the content of this conversation include?

DETECTIVE

What was your relationship like with Sheriff?

BUTLER

Why? What did you hear?

DETECTIVE

What makes you think I heard anything?

BUTLER

I'm not fatuous. I have observed you approaching each individual in interrogation. I'm sure someone mentioned that Sheriff married Administrative.

DETECTIVE

Yes. Where is she, by the way?

BUTLER

Business trip. And I truly have forgiven him. So, to answer your question I did not shoot the Sheriff. Besides, it is difficult to remain irate with someone as courteous as Sheriff.

DETECTIVE

What do you mean? He stole your girlfriend.

BUTLER

When we were children, I made a foolish mistake. One day Bully, one of the town tyrants asked me what I would do for a Klondike Bar. I really wanted that Klondike Bar. So, I went skinny dipping in the lake. When I came out Bully ran away with my clothes. Sheriff gave me his shorts and walked me all the way home. It was a dreadful thing to see us. Two boys walking home one wearing nothing but a pair of shorts and the other wearing a t-shirt, underwear, and sandals. Not only did he lend me his shorts, but he gave me a Klondike Bar, a bar I never received from Bully. He has always brought wonderful companionship to our relationship. His only mistake was when he married Administrative. But I forgave him and Administrative. However, I do not believe Maid has forgiven him.

DETECTIVE

Excuse me?

BUTLER

She despises him. You notice how she kept mentioning that Sheriff is Wife's father-in-law? *(DETECTIVE nods yes)*. Well, Maid is envious that Sheriff loves Wife more. *(Beat)* You see, years ago Sheriff cheated on

Administrative with Waitress. Maid is their love child. Administrative never knew, but Waitress made Sheriff see his daughter. The only way Sheriff knew he could keep Maid in his life without his wife being aware of Waitress was to have Maid labor for him. So when she became the age of seventeen she commenced to labor for Sheriff, but he still never treated her like his daughter. I believe she shot him in anger.

DETECTIVE

I don't believe this. Thank you.

BUTLER

You are welcome.

DETECTIVE

(GARDENER *exits to back yard (garden).* BABY GIRL *enters with Klondike Bar and returns to spot in front of the television.* DETECTIVE *walks towards* MAID). Hello. May I speak with you?

MAID

Sure. Did ya find out who shot 'em yet?

DETECTIVE

No. Not even close. So, tell me about your relationship with Sheriff.

MAID

Well, there is nuttin' much ta say. He and my mother were really close friends. When she died from a squirrel attack, he helped me pay for her funeral and he even let me live wit 'em. I love him. I really do. I just can't believe Pool Boy shot 'em.

DETECTIVE

Pool Boy Shot him?

MAID

Yeah, it's so obvious. Last week Sheriff caught Pool Boy swimming instead of cleaning the pool one day and Sheriff gave 'em a good ol' fashion spankin'. Pool Boy was very furious about the spankin'. He said he would kill 'em when he gets the chance.

DETECTIVE

Well, thank you for the information.

MAID

Yes sir.

DETECTIVE

(POOL BOY enters wet. He wipes himself off with a beach towel. DETECTIVE walks towards POOL BOY. COOK exits to kitchen). Hey Pool Boy, how are you?

POOL BOY

Totally awesome dude.

DETECTIVE

Explain to me why you would not shoot Sheriff. I'm trying to narrow this down.

POOL BOY

Sheriff is a great dude, dude. He gives me money when I ask for it. If I shoot him that's the end of the money. I work for Husband, so any extra money I want I get it from Sheriff.

DETECTIVE

Do you have an idea who shot him?

POOL BOY

Yeah Dude, Cook blasted him.

DETECTIVE

And why do you think that?

POOL BOY

Because she's a thug. She shoots people. *(He walks away to the bathroom. As he enters he reacts badly to the bleach smell. He walks away).*

DETECTIVE

(To himself) Well, here I am back at square one. Everyone has a motive and everyone thinks someone else did it. How can I narrow it down to one? Who in here is unbiased? *(GARDENER enters with a batch of strawberries in one hand and an apple in the other. He takes a bite out of the apple and shares the strawberries with WIFE. DETECTIVE looks over at BABY GIRL. He walks towards her).* Hello, Baby Girl, may I talk to you?

BABY GIRL

Sure.

DETECTIVE

What do you think about all that is going on?

BABY GIRL

It's just horrible. My gramps is a wonderful man. It's a shame Burglar shot him

DETECTIVE

Who's Burglar.

BABY GIRL

Oh, he is a mean man. He's been on the news the past couple of weeks. He burglared the supermarket, he burglared the gas station, and he burglared the bank. I think he knows my gramps is rich so he came here to burglar my gramps too. He came through the window and shot gramps. Then he escaped through the window. I don't know where he is, but if you can find him, I would greatly appreciate it.

DETECTIVE

I will do that. Just for you.

BABY GIRL

Thank you (COOK *enters with two Klondike bars. She offers one to* BUTLER, *he covers himself as if he is naked. In confusion she shrugs her shoulder and offers it to* MAID. MAID *takes one and* COOK *eats the other*).

DETECTIVE

Well, that didn't help any. I guess, I'll go upstairs and find some more evidence. *(He exits upstairs. Blackout)*

ACT ONE SCENE FOUR

All are still watching the television. DETECTIVE *enters from upstairs.*

GARDENER

Did you find anything?

DETECTIVE

Maybe. Wife, do you mind if I use your phone?

WIFE

Not at all.

DETECTIVE

(Picks up phone and dials) Hello, Hi. This is Detective. Yes. I need you to do me a favor. *(Whispering)* I need you to do a background check on the following people for me. You have a pen and paper? Okay, you ready? Alright, the names are Wife, Gardener, Maid, Pool Boy, Cook, Butler, and Nurse. Okay? I need an extensive research done, okay. And when you're done can you send it to me? *(Pause)* Oh, right, of course. Um…oh, maybe you can fax it to me. Hold on, let me ask. Wife do you have a fax machine.

WIFE

Yes.

DETECTIVE

Perfect. Yes, there's a fax machine here. Oh, yeah, of course, hold on again. Wife what's the fax number?

WIFE

732

DETECTIVE

732

WIFE

867

DETECTIVE

867

WIFE

5309

DETECTIVE

5309. Okay, that's 7-3-2. 8-6-7-5-3-0-9. Okay, please send it as soon as possible. Thank you, Assistant. *(Hangs up phone)*. Okay, this is perfect.

BUTLER

Are you any closer to solving the case?

DETECTIVE

Of course. Well, not exactly. Well, I think so. No.

MAID

How long is this gonna take?

DETECTIVE

Why? Are you in a hurry to leave?

MAID

No. I got work ta do. This ain't gonna take all night, is it?

DETECTIVE

I don't know. You know it would be over if one of you would just confess.

Simultaneously

POOL BOY: Dude, I didn't do it.

GARDENER: I no shoot him.

WIFE: I did not shoot my father-in-law.

COOK: I didn't cap his ass.

BUTLER: I could never shoot him.

NURSE: I totally did not shoot him.

MAID: Sir, I's promise ya, I did no sucha thing.

DETECTIVE

None of you shot him, but yet you were the only ones in the house.

GARDENER

I was outside in the garden.

POOL BOY

I was in the pool…cleaning the pool.

WIFE

I was at the supermarket.

DETECTIVE

You know what; let's not talk about this right now. I have some paper work coming over that will help the case. Until they fax them there's not much I can do. So, let's just not talk about it until they come.

COOK

Yo, I can do that.

BUTLER

I have not observed any problem in the conclusion of your decision.

DETECTIVE

Good. *(There is a long moment of silence).* So, what do you guys want to talk about?

POOL BOY

Dude, the TV is on. How 'bout we just watch TV.

DETECTIVE

Okay. *(Another pause).* So, what do you guys want to watch?

BABY GIRL

Well, I'm watching *Sesame Seeds Street*.

DETECTIVE

Well, that's fine. *(Another pause).* So, is anyone hungry?

POOL BOY

Very.

MAID

I sure could nibble on summin'.

COOK

Did ya'll want me ta cook sum'in?

WIFE

That would be a great idea. That's if, of course, Detective is okay with it.

DETECTIVE

Yeah, that's fine. *(COOK exits. Another pause).* So, what do you think of Obama? Change of history, right?

WIFE

Yes.

GARDENER

él muy buen.

MAID

I'm glad I got ta see it happen.

POOL BOY

He ain't all that.

NURSE

His wife like totally uses my designer.

BUTLER

Inspiring.

BABY GIRL

Is that the dead guy?

DETECTIVE

No, that's Osama. We're talking about Obama, the president.

WIFE

Can we just watch the TV in silence?

DETECTIVE

Sure. *(Pause)* So, did anyone watch the game last night?

POOL BOY

Which one?

DETECTIVE

Is there more than one?

MAID

Which sport ya talkin' 'bout, baby?

DETECTIVE

I don't know just trying to make conversation.

BUTLER

Select another topic.

DETECTIVE

(Pause) So, what do you think about the Jersey Shore?

POOL BOY

Dude, it's totally awesome.

MAID

I hate it. It's one hundred percent garbage.

NURSE

Like how could you hate it? It totally has like some of the best beaches in America. And they may have garbage on them, but what beach doesn't

MAID

Oh, I thought you were talking about the TV show. Not the actual shore.

DETECTIVE

There's a TV show about the shore. What is it about?

GARDENER

Nothing really.

NURSE

It's totally about a bunch of girls and boys getting down at the shore.

MAID

It's trash. All they do is show all of the sluts of New Joisey.

WIFE

Are you talking about the Housewives of New Jersey?

MAID

No.

POOL BOY

That's not all they show. They also show the thugs of New Yawk.

WIFE

Are you talking about the Housewives of New York?

POOL BOY

No.

MAID

We talkin' 'bout a show called Jersey Show. It's a reality show on MTV. All theys do is show a bunch-a sex crazed boys who come from New York ta have sex with the sluts of New Jersey.

WIFE

So it's a reality show about politicians?

NURSE

Like no.

BUTLER

Can we not discuss this matter any more? Besides we all came to the agreement to watch television in silence.

DETECTIVE

(*Pause. Thinking of another subject, finally he gives up. Within seconds he begins to unconsciously sing*). On top of spaghetti--

POOL BOY

(*Unconsciously singing*) All covered in cheese.

DETECTIVE and POOL BOY

I lost my poor meatball-

GARDENER

In somebody's sleeves.

MAID

What? It's when somebody sneezed.

GARDENER

Oh, I'm sorry.

DETECTIVE

(Pause. Begins to sing again). This is the song that doesn't end.

BUTLER

It just goes on and on my friend.

MAID

Some people started sanging it not knowin' what it was.

NURSE

And they totally continued signing it like forever just because this totally is like the song that really totally doesn't end.

DETECTIVE

You just totally ruined the song.

WIFE

I thought we agreed to watch the television in silence.

DETECTIVE

I don't know if that's a good idea.

WIFE

Why not?

DETECTIVE

Because, the audience might get board.

WIFE

Well, what else are we supposed to talk about?

BUTLER

Why are we ignoring the obvious? Shouldn't we be discussing who shot Sheriff?

GARDENER

I thought we decided not to talk about that until the fax came in.

DETECTIVE

Yes, we did, but I do not know how long that will be. You know, you would all make my job much easier if you would just confess.

GARDENER

Maybe Cook did it. She probably escaped from the kitchen door.

DETECTIVE

She wouldn't do that.

BUTLER

She sure would, if she shot him.

DETECTIVE

Cook! Cook! Get in here. *(No response)* Oh my gosh she ran away. *(He goes to exit, Cook enters).*

COOK

What the hell is ya'll yelling for?

DETECTIVE

Oh, good you didn't leave. Everyone thought you tried to make an escape.

COOK

WHAT THE PEBBLES!

DETECTIVE

They thought that you shot him and then tried to escape through the door in the kitchen.

COOK

Ya'll accuse me behind my back? I should shoot ya'll. *(Beat)* I did not shoot Sheriff.

DETECTIVE

Well, what about the rest of you.

BUTLER

I don't even have a gun.

DETECTIVE

The gun used was Sheriff's.

MAID

That thang is locked up. And I ain't gots the password for it. So, that let's ya'll know I didn't shoot 'em.

BABY GIRL

Not necessarily. Gramps keeps many things in the safe. He could have opened it and the shooter could have taken the gun. *(Everyone looks at her in suspension).* It's just a guess. And no, I did not shoot gramps. I was in school.

POOL BOY

I wouldn't shoot him. I couldn't shoot him. I did not shoot him.

WIFE

I could never shoot my father

MAID

In-law, father-in-law.

WIFE

Why do you keep insinuating that I shot my father?

MAID

I ain't insinuating that you shot your father-*in-law*.

WIFE

(Frustrated) You are insinuating.

MAID

I ain't insinuating.

WIFE

You are too insinuating!

DETECTIVE

Okay that is enough. Insinuating is a word added to the list of words you cannot use. In fact you cannot use any words that begin with the letter "I." And that goes for everyone. No one may use any word that begins with the letter "I."

WIFE

That is insane.

DETECTIVE

What did me just say?

WIFE

That be ridiculous.

BUTLER

You cannot be serious Detective.

DETECTIVE

Me be very serious.

COOK

Detective, you have lost your damn mind.

DETECTIVE

Can you blame me? Me've been hanging around the likes of you people. Going back and forth about how you didn't shoot the Sheriff, but yet he has been shot. *(Pouting)* Now one of you shot him and one of you better tell me who shot him.

NURSE

Like we should all totally take a lie detector test.

COOK

Where the hell we gonna get the machine from?

NURSE

Well, like maybe someone can like totally fax the thing over.

BUTLER

Me would gladly take the test to prove that myself did not shoot him.

POOL BOY

Me cannot believe this be going on right now.

GARDENER

Esto es estúpido.

COOK

Me about to shoot somebody.

WIFE

Me can't believe we are actually using sentences without "I" words.

BUTLER

Can we please venture back to using words that begin with the letter "I"?

DETECTIVE

Absolutely not.

WIFE

How will this solve the answer of who shot my dad?

MAID

Your dad by-law.

WIFE

Me be getting sick of you suggesting that me shot my dad.

MAID

Me ain't suggesting nothing. Me just pointing out the fact that Sheriff be your father-by-law and not your father.

COOK

Would you two please shut up?

WIFE

Me won't shut up until Maid stops suggesting me shot Sheriff.

DETECTIVE

Okay new rule. Wife and Maid, you two may not speak to each other until we figure out who shot the Sheriff. Now, Cook, go back to the kitchen and continue cooking. Me be hungry. *(Cook exits)*.

WIFE

How much longer will this take?

DETECTIVE

There's only 12 pages left of the script.

WIFE

Oh, thank God. Me don't know how much longer me can speak without "I" words.

DETECTIVE

(Fax rings). What's that?

WIFE

That be the fax machine.

DETECTIVE

Oh great. *(Thinking hard while saying sentence without "I" words)*. What room…does the machine be located?

WIFE

The fax be located…um…be located …uh…it's, I mean, um… damn it, it's in the den. *(DETECTIVE exits).* This is just ridiculous.

NURSE

Ooh, me telling. You're totally not supposed to use "I words." Like totally.

WIFE

This is my house. I can do whatever the hell I want.

COOK

(Enters). The food be just about ready. Butler you might want to set the table.

BUTLER

Me will do that. *(Exits).*

DETECTIVE

(Enters with pages and pages of faxes. He's reading them as he enters). Oh my goodness. Me don't believe that. What? Are you serious? You have to be kidding me? Oh my gosh. Really? No. Me don't believe what me be reading.

GARDENER

What be that?

DETECTIVE

Just some vital data that me needed.

WIFE

Will this data solve the case? I want to know who shot my daddy.

MAID

You're daddy-by-law.

WIFE

I thought Detective said you were not supposed to talk to me.

MAID

Me thought detective said you were not supposed to use "I" words.

DETECTIVE

(Pouting) Ladies, please stop. *(New idea)* How about this. We will all go to the dinning room and eat. After we eat we will return and me will solve the case.

POOL BOY

That's bodacious dude.

NURSE

Yeah, me totally be hungry. Me haven't eaten like all day.

GARDENER

Mi quiero Taco Bell.

COOK

(Every one exits to dining room). Pool Boy, can you help me bring out the food me cooked? *(POOL BOY agrees. Both exit to kitchen)*

DETECTIVE

(DETECTIVE places his pages of faxes on a table. As he does so the phone rings. He answers it). Hello, Husband and Wife residents, how may me direct your call? *(Slight pause)* Oh, she's not available may me ask who be calling? *(Pause).* Oh, did you want me to take a message? *(Beat)* Ok. *(Pause).* Really. Are you serious? Oh my word. Okay. Me will give the message as soon as me sees her. Okay, have a great day. Bye. *(Hangs up phone)* Well, would you look at that? *(POOL BOY enters with Taco Bell and then exits to dining room. As DETECTIVE proceeds to exit his cell phone rings).* Hello. Speaking. *(Pause).* Oh really. What did he say? Seriously? Wow. That be amazing. Sure. Me will let them know. Me'll be down there soon. Okay. Bye. *(Hangs up phone)* Oh my goodness. Cook!

COOK

(Enters with a pizza box and soda) Yes, Detective.

DETECTIVE

Me need you to go to the dinning room and tell everyone to come here.

COOK

Um…okay. *(Exits to dining room)*

WIFE

(Soon everyone enters) Detective what is going on?

NURSE

No "I" words, Wife.

WIFE

Okay that's enough with the stupid restrictions. This is my house and I have declared that it is now okay to use "I" words.

DETECTIVE

Alright, we can all use "I" words once again. Everyone gather 'round. I have good news. And it has nothing to with car insurance.

COOK

Well, what *is it*?

DETECTIVE

Me, I mean, I…I have found out who shot the Sheriff.

WIFE

Oh, that's great. Well, who did it?

DETECTIVE

You all had great motive to do it, but only one of you did it.

MAID

Well, yeah, we know that. Who did it?

                          DETECTIVE

Do you really want to know?

                            WIFE

Yes.

                          DETECTIVE

Are you sure?

                          POOL BOY

Yeah, dude. Hurry up.

                          DETECTIVE

Are you positive?

                            COOK

Detective, if you don't say it Imma shoot you.

                          DETECTIVE

Do you really want to-?

                            ALL

JUST SAY IT!

                          DETECTIVE

Sure thing. But not until after this little break. Ladies

                      NURSE, MAID, COOK

(Stand in girl group formation and sing). After this little break, we'll be right back.

(Blackout)

ACT ONE SCENE FIVE

This scene opens with every one sitting except DETECTIVE.

WIFE

Detective, I wish you would hurry up and tell us who shot my daddy.

MAID

Your daddy-in-

ALL

Shut up, Maid!

DETECTIVE

Speaking of the Maid. Maid.

MAID

Yes sir.

DETECTIVE

Why are you so concern to let everyone know that Sheriff is Wife's father-in-law? Are you jealous of Wife?

MAID

No. Why would I be jealous?

DETECTIVE

Because you are upset that Sheriff treats Wife more like a daughter then he treats you.

GARDENER

Why would he treat Maid like a daughter to begin with? It's not like Maid is his daughter.

MAID

I AM TOO.

DETECTIVE

Ah-ha.

WIFE

WHAT? How can that be?

DETECTIVE

Sheriff had an affair and Maid is the result of it.

COOK

Well, damn.

MAID

Yeah, it's true. I'm his daughter. And he loves me more than you Wife. Always remember that. I will always be his daughter. Always!

DETECTIVE

And that was your motive to shoot him. You hated the fact that he loves Wife more than you.

MAID

If I was gonna shoot anyone it woulda been Wife.

DETECTIVE

Exactly. And that's why you did not shoot the Sheriff. Wife.

WIFE

I didn't shoot him.

DETECTIVE

Didn't you try to have Sheriff moved to a nursing home?

WIFE

Because, they could take care of him better then I could. That's the only reason. I was not trying to get rid of him.

DETECTIVE

Then why did you try to drown him a week earlier?

WIFE

That was an accident. How did you know about that?

DETECTIVE

The faxes I received told me a lot about you guys. Now why did you try to drown him?

WIFE

I didn't try to drown him. When he told me he wanted to go swimming, I took him to the pool. I did not realize he was sedated and was talking to his imaginary friend Pascal. If I knew that I would have never taken him into the pool. I truly love my father-in-law. I wouldn't shoot him. Besides, I was at the supermarket.

DETECTIVE

I know that's why you didn't shoot him. Butler. Isn't it true that Sheriff's wife used to be your girlfriend? And you haven't forgiven him yet, have you?

BUTLER

Yes, me have. And yes that be a motive, but me promise you me did not shoot him.

COOK

You can use "I" words now.

BUTLER

Sorry, I forgot.

DETECTIVE

Yeah, I know, you didn't shoot him either. Cook.

COOK

What is you gonna do, accuse everyone until you get to the shooter?

DETECTIVE

Yes. Cook, isn't it true that you did some jail time?

COOK

Yeah. So.

DETECTIVE

You've been to jail six times. Can you tell everyone what you went to jail for the sixth time?

COOK

I…I shot a man…in the ear.

BUTLER

So, you did shoot him.

COOK

I didn't shoot Sheriff. My past has nothing to do with my present. Besides, there was no time for me to shoot him and then end up in the kitchen.

DETECTIVE

You could have gone out the window and then ran to the kitchen door.

COOK

But Pool Boy or Gardener would have seen me.

DETECTIVE

I know that's why you didn't shoot him. Gardener, isn't it true that you and Sheriff recently had an argument over you getting a raise?

GARDENER

Yes, but I wouldn't shoot him over a raise.

DETECTIVE

No. But you are in this country illegally, aren't you? And Sheriff threatened you, didn't he? Sheriff had all the power to get you shipped back. And you were afraid so you shot him.

GARDENER

Yes. No. Yes, I mean, yes, he threatened me, but I wouldn't shoot him. Besides, it's not like we're in Arizona.

DETECTIVE

I know. Nurse.

NURSE

Like what?

DETECTIVE

Isn't it true that Sheriff was mistreating you?

NURSE

He like totally didn't mean any harm. Besides he's totally sedated half the time. He doesn't know what he's doing.

DETECTIVE

But that didn't stop you from getting upset and shooting him.

NURSE

As if. I did not shoot him. Besides I never held a gun in my life.

DETECTIVE

Oh no. What about the super soaker you use to lose the "Best at Aim Water Gun Shoot." You came in dead last making you a perfect candidate.

NURSE

That was totally just for shittles and giggles. I would totally never shoot anyone for real.

DETECTIVE

Of course not. That's why you didn't shoot him either.

WIFE

Well, that only leaves one other person.

ALL

Pool Boy.

POOL BOY

I didn't shoot him.

DETECTIVE

Pool Boy, isn't it true that Sheriff gave you a spanking?

POOL BOY

Yes, and it still hurts to sit, but I wouldn't shoot him over that.

DETECTIVE

I know.

MAID

This isn't making any sense. There is no one left.

BUTLER

Detective, have you realized yet, that you are wasting time.

WIFE

And spreading all of our dirty laundry. The audience did not need to know all of that information.

DETECTIVE

There is one suspect left. *(Slight pause. Everyone looks around)* Baby Girl.

ALL

(Gasp) Baby Girl?

DETECTIVE

Yes, Baby Girl.

WIFE

Now, stop it. Detective you have gone too far. Baby Girl did not shoot him. Besides she was in school all day.

DETECTIVE

I have a question for you Baby Girl. When you entered the house today why were you wearing a scarf and gloves when it is in the middle of summer?

NURSE

Yeah, I just like totally noticed that.

BABY GIRL

Well, Detective the air condition in my school gets so high that it gets so cold. So I bring a scarf and gloves. It's so I stay comfortable while I am in school. It's difficult to learn when you are freezing.

DETECTIVE

Oh really. Were you even in school Baby Girl?

BABY GIRL

Yes, Detective.

DETECTIVE

Then tell me; what did you do in class today?

WIFE

Oh please, don't start that again. I told you before she doesn't know what Algebra is.

BABY GIRL

Yes I do mommy, it's annoying.

DETECTIVE

Are you sure you were in school, Baby Girl?

BABY GIRL

(Frustrated) Yes, Detective.

DETECTIVE

Oh really. Wife, when you guys left to the dining room Principal called and I took a message for you.

WIFE

(DETECTIVE hands WIFE the message, she reads it). Wife, this is Principal. Just called to see if everything is okay with Baby Girl. She was absent all day today and you or Husband did not call to release her today. Please call back as soon as possible. Thank you. *(To BABY GIRL)* Oh, my goodness, Baby Girl is this true?

BABY GIRL

No, mommy. They must have gotten me mistaken with someone else.

DETECTIVE

Oh really, then why did I find a piece of fabric from your scarf in Sheriff's room?

BABY GIRL

I go in there all the time. I'm sure many of my stuff shows up in there.

DETECTIVE

Even on the window where the shooter escaped? And when I was talking to you earlier, how did you know the shooter used the window to escape?

BABY GIRL

Uh…because you said so.

COOK

Yeah, man, you told us that.

DETECTIVE

Yes, I did, but Baby Girl wasn't here when I said it.

BABY GIRL

Oh, then it was guess.

DETECTIVE

No, it wasn't a guess. You shot Sheriff.

BABY GIRL

(They all gasp) No, I didn't, honestly, I didn't.

DETECTIVE

This is what happened. First, you waited until your mother left and everyone was out of sight. Second, you went into his room, punched in the code to the safe, took the gun and shot him. Third, you escaped the window using your scarf. You then hid so neither Gardener or Pool Boy would see you. Fourth, you then waited until Gardener and Pool Boy left, and then you ran far away and came back just in time to make everyone think you were in school.

BABY GIRL

That's not true and you have no proof.

BUTLER

And she doesn't even have the password for the safe.

WIFE

Yes she does, gramps gave it to her.

BABY GIRL

Shut up, mother!

COOK

But there's no motive.

DETECTIVE

This is a play we don't need a motive.

WIFE

There is still no hard evidence. I'm not going to have you accusing Baby Girl of such horrendous actions. You have completely lost your mind. Please leave my house.

DETECTIVE

I have one last huge piece of evidence that proves Baby Girl shot the Sheriff.

BUTLER

And what might that be?

DETECTIVE

I got a call on my cell phone from the hospital. Sheriff awoke and said Baby Girl shot him.

BABY GIRL

I didn't shoot him.

DETECTIVE

You did to.

BABY GIRL

(Louder) I didn't shoot him.

DETECTIVE

(Louder) You did to.

BABY GIRL

I DID NOT SHOOT HIM!

DETECTIVE

YOU DID TO!

BABY GIRL

Okay, okay, okay. I shot the Sheriff, but I did not shoot the deputy. *(To the audience)* Ya'll was waiting all night for that, weren't you?

WIFE

NOOOOOOOOOOOOOOOOOOO! Baby Girl, how could you shoot grandpa? I can't believe Baby Girl did such a bad thing.

BABY GIRL

Get over it.

DETECTIVE

Well, it's time for you to go to jail. *(Calls).* Cop.

COP

(Enters) Yes, Detective.

DETECTIVE

It's time to arrest the shooter of the Sheriff.

COP

Okay. *(Walks towards BABY GIRL).* Let's go shooter.

DETECTIVE

Wait a second. How did you know she was the shooter?

COP

I heard everything from backstage. *(Handcuffs BABY GIRL).*

BABY GIRL

That's alright. You haven't heard or seen the last of me. I'm going to get you; I'm going to get you all. *(BABY GIRL bursts into the "evil laugh" COP and BABY GIRL go to exit).*

WIFE

Wait a second.

DETECTIVE

What's wrong?

WIFE

The show is about to end and we don't have a moral or even a message.

NURSE

Like what do you totally mean?

WIFE

Every play has to have a moral or a message so the audience goes home thinking differently about life. We're not just supposed to entertain them, but we are to educate them about life and the meaning of life. We need a moral or message.

BUTLER

Well, isn't the playwright supposed to have written it already in the script?

WIFE

Yes, but this playwright has not.

COOK

You know, playwrights can be so damn annoying sometimes.

WIFE

Yes, just like Algebra, but either or we need a message. So, start thinking.

POOL BOY

Yo, dude, I got one. You shouldn't shoot people.

WIFE

No, that's too boring.

NURSE

Like you totally shouldn't lie about shooting people.

WIFE

No, that's even more boringer.

MAID

You shouldn't get caught shootin' peoples.

BABY GIRL

You shouldn't skip school.

BUTLER

You shouldn't steal your friend's girlfriend.

COOK

(Not sure) You shouldn't go to the supermarket on a Monday morning?

WIFE

No, keep thinking

DETECTIVE

No matter what bad thing you do in life, in the end you will always get caught.

WIFE

No, no, NO. Come on now, think better.

BUTLER

Well, how can any of us think? We are all famished. We haven't dined all day.

WIFE

That's it, that's the message.

MAID

What?

WIFE

Never think on an empty stomach. *(Everyone adlibs and applauds in agreement).* Okay, we have our message for the audience.

DETECTIVE

Good. Okay, Cop, take her to jail. *(COP and BABY GIRL exit).* Well, my work here is done. It was nice meeting all of you weird, demented, and crazy people. It is time for me to go. *(Exits)*

MAID

Wow, that is just horrible. Who woulda thought such an innocent girl would do sucha thang.

BUTLER

It is very depressing.

NURSE

It's like totally heart breaking.

POOL BOY

Dude, my tears fall for her.

WIFE

I can't believe my baby is going to jail.

GARDENER

I pray she gets the help she needs.

COOK

(Pause) Well…dinner's ready.

Simultaneously

BUTLER: Oh, good, because I'm hungry

MAID: Yes, Lawd. It's time to eat

GARDENER: Thank God, I thought we would never eat.

NURSE: Like totally awesome.

WIFE: Oh good, let's go eat.

POOL BOY: I am starving, dude.

COOK

I made some really good tacos. *(Everyone exits to dining room)*

CURTAINS

Maria's Troupe

CASEY BELL

Maria's Troupe

Copyright ©2008 Casey Bell

All rights reserved. No part of this publication may be reproduced, stored in a retrieval system or transmitted in any form or by any means, electronic, mechanical, photocopying, recording or otherwise, without the prior written permission of the publisher.

Published by: BookCase Publishing

Cover Design by Casey Bell

Printed in the United States

Casey Bell
PO Box 5231
Old Bridge, NJ 08857
caseysamuelbell.com
authorcaseybell.com
readywritercsb.com

MARIA'S TROUPE©

By: Casey Bell

CHARACTERS:

MARIA BALLARD: She is the director of the production. Age: 36.

BRIAN: He is the stage manager. Age range: 25-30.

VIOLA STEPHANIE: She is the playwright of the play. Age range: 35-40.

ANTHONY BRIDGES: He is a reviewer. Age: 37.

CLAIR: Age: 25. She plays Vicky Johnson, Aaron's mother, Robert's wife.

ALEX: Age: 30. He plays Robert Johnson, Aaron's father, Vicky's husband.

JOHN: Age: 18. He plays Aaron Johnson, Vicky and Robert's son.

SARAH: Age range: 26. She plays Elizabeth (Lizzie), and Aunt Gloria.

GREG: Age range: 18-25. He plays Jason.

JILL: Age range: 20-25. She plays the doctor, and Grandma.

USHER

AUDIENCE MEMBERS (1 MAN, 1 WOMAN)

EXTRAS: Includes Uncle Jacob, audience members, rave, party, family, and friends. 6 min.

ACT ONE SCENE ONE

This scene takes place four days before opening night.

ANTHONY

(When the lights come up ANTHONY and MARIA are sitting across from each other. They are sitting at a table, which is a part of the set). I want to thank you for allowing me to interview you.

MARIA

Oh, no problem. So, ask me all the questions you want.

ANTHONY

First things first. Why "The Party Stops Here?" It is one of Viola's oldest play, and noone likes it. Is there a reason why you chose it.

MARIA

I know how much everyone dislikes it, but I enjoy it a lot. When I read it I knew I had to direct it one day. I'm really glad to do this production. Not only is it a good script, it teaches mankind of good and evil. I enjoy this play because it educates and entertains. *(Laughs)* Listen to me babble on. You must be sick of me.

ANTHONY

Oh, no. I enjoy interviewing someone who has a lot to say. It gives me a lot to write about. So, tell me about this fund-raising project you're doing.

MARIA

Oh, you must mean the Make-A-Wish Foundation. I've decided to give half of our profits to the Make-A-Wish foundation. I think it's time that all businesses, organizations and companies share their funds with different programs. Next year I plan on donating to the Breast Cancer Awareness Center.

ANTHONY

That is so nice of you. One last question. Is there something you would like to do that you have never done before in this business?

MARIA

Well, there is this one thing. I really enjoy Viola Stephanie as a playwright. I would love to collaborate with her one day. *(Speaking as if she is in a dream)* You know, direct one of her new plays with her by my side. Guiding me as I direct her piece of art. Making her words on the page a miraculous work on stage. It's a dream I've had ever since I read her first play Roger & Julia. *(Returns from outer space)* Of course that's just a silly dream, but , there's nothing wrong with dreaming.

ANTHONY

Wow, that's great. Well, thanks for the interview *(stands)*.

MARIA

(Stands) No problem.

ANTHONY

Now, I'll be here opening night to write the review. I hope you guys break all legs.

MARIA

I hope so too. I'm so afraid that opening night will go wrong.

ANTHONY

Don't worry about it. If your directing skills are as good as your looks, then you have nothing to worry about.

MARIA

(Blushes) Oh, please. You don't mean that.

ANTHONY

I mean every word. *(Beat)* It was nice meeting you, Maria *(They shake hands. He holds on and looks into her eyes, he then let goes, he exits. MARIA stands their smiling, with her hand out as if ANTHONY is still there).*

SARAH

(Enters, approaches MARIA) Maria *(no response)* Maria *(no response)* Maria! *(Claps hands)*

MARIA

(Snaps out of it) Oh, Sarah, hi. What's wrong?

SARAH

What time are we starting?

MARIA

(Looks at watch) Oh, right now. Tell everyone to get into place. Thank you. Oh one more thing, can you get someone to help you move the table and chairs off the stage. Thank you. *(SARAH exits, MARIA walks toward directing table. SARAH and ALEX enter, they exit with table and chairs, JOHN, and party extras enter).* Lights!

GREG

(Blackout occurs, few seconds later lights and music come up; speaking to JOHN) Hey Aaron, isn't this party great. *(JOHN nods, pauses, then collapses. Everyone rushes over and panics)* Aaron, what's wrong? *(Kneels down and listens to JOHN's stomach)* Oh my gosh he's not breathing. *The crowd goes silent).* Someone call 911.

SARAH

(SARAH takes her cellular phone and dials). Hello, my name is Liz—Lesley Higgins and I have a problem. There's this kid and he's not breathing. *(Pause)* I don't know how he stopped breathing, I just know he's not breathing. *(Pause)* Who cares about all of that, just get someone here fast. *(Pause)* We're by the old warehouse on Morris drive; please hurry.

GREG

(He asks one of the party extras to watch over him (JOHN); then he walks towards SARAH) Why did you lie about your name?

SARAH

If the police find out what he was doing, there's a big chance we are going to get in trouble. I can't get in trouble; it would hurt me and my families' name.

GREG

So you rather worry about your reputation than someone else's life?

SARAH

What do you care, just make sure he doesn't die.

GREG

Well, the police should be here any minute

SARAH

Well, I'm leaving.

GREG

Where are you going?

SARAH

I don't wanna be here when the cops get here. I'll see you tomorrow by Lakeland Ave, that's where Houston's rave is. Jason, don't bring the chump *(exits)*.

GREG

Lizzie, you can't leave me here *(police sirens are heard; the rave extra's disperse. GREG kneels down to JOHN).* I'm sorry buddy. *(Blackout)*

MARIA

(Lights come back up) That was good guys. Let's continue with the next scene please.

BRIAN

(Enters; has cellular phone to his ear. He has a book bag and a Starbucks cup in his hand). I'll call you later, okay. Bye. *(Walks SL towards MARIA; hangs up phone)*

MARIA

You're late.

BRIAN

Yes I know. I went to Starbucks and the line was crazy. I thought to myself I should probably leave or I'll be late, but then I thought, I really want my French Vanilla drink, so I decided to wait in line for it *(sips drinks)* and it is good.

MARIA

Well, you could have called and told me you were going to be late.

BRIAN

I know, but I didn't feel like it. *(Beat)* So what's going on.

MARIA

We are starting act one scene two.

BRIAN

That's as far as you got?

MARIA

Yes. We would have gone further, but we waited about fifteen minutes for you. When we realized you weren't coming, we started without you.

BRIAN

Well, I was coming, I just had to go to Starbucks.

MARIA

Brian, as a stage manager it is your job to be here early. You're supposed to set an example for everyone else.

BRIAN

I know, but Starbucks.

MARIA

(Frustrated) I am not about to argue with you.

BRIAN

You don't have to argue, all I was saying was–

MARIA

Be quiet, the scene is about to start

CLAIR

(A blackout occurs for 2-3 seconds. When the lights come back up CLAIR enters. She looks over at JOHN and starts to cry; she walks toward JOHN) Aaron. Aaron, please speak to me. How could you do this to yourself? Why were you hanging around that crowd? *(Pause; kneels down to JOHN and embraces him)* Aaron, please don't die.

ALEX

(CLAIR weeps, ALEX enters and sees CLAIR, and he puts his head down, takes a deep breath and walks towards CLAIR). Honey *(CLAIR gets up and runs to ALEX and they embrace)* Vicky, the doctor said he'll be okay.

CLAIR

(She let goes of ALEX.) We don't know that. Look at him. Robert look at him *(ALEX looks at him).* Does that look like he's going to be okay?

ALEX

Looks can be deceiving. Many people make miraculous recoveries.

CLAIR

This is our fault. We should have been stricter.

ALEX

Honey, don't start putting blame on anyone. No one could have prepared for anything like this. The only thing we can do is wait *(dramatic pause)* and pray. *(Blackout)*

MARIA

That was great. Please go on.

BRIAN

(JOHN, CLAIR, and ALEX exit the stage. GREG, SARAH, and extras set up for the next scene). GREG sits in the middle of the "couch" (The couch are three chairs side by side draped with a blanket). SARAH sits next to him; the extras are sitting on the floor, chairs, or standing around a counter/bar. Lights come up, there's party music playing quietly in the background). What the hell are they sitting on?

MARIA

I couldn't afford a couch.

BRIAN

That's ghetto, and it's not gonna work. I can already see something wrong happening with those chairs.

MARIA

Brian, keep it quiet.

GREG

I can't believe he just collapsed. I feel bad; I could have killed him.

SARAH

Jason, none of this is your fault. Aaron chose to take X, and drink all that beer. No one forced him.

GREG

But, I suggested he take it to get comfortable. If I didn't suggest it, he wouldn't have taken it.

SARAH

Well, what's done is done. Don't go beating yourself up for what someone else did to themselves.

GREG

Lizzie. We have to stop doing this. This was a sign. If it happened to him, it could happen to us.

SARAH

Greg, don't go soft on me. *(Picks up a beer from the bar)* Come on, suck it up *(hands him a drink)* have a beer.

GREG

No. *(Stands up)* I need to go for a walk to clear my head. *(He exits the stage. Blackout).*

GREG

(Lights come up. JOHN is lying on the bed and GREG is sitting on a chair besides him. GREG is crying). This is my fault. Why, did I suggest you take those pills?

CLAIR

(CLAIR and ALEX enter. They both look at GREG strangely). Who are you? How do you know my son?

GREG

(He looks up at them) Oh, you're his parents? My name is Jason. I was his friend; we hung out a lot.

CLAIR

(Angry) Are you one of the friends who got him in this state?

GREG

(Hesitant) I...I'm not sure what–

CLAIR

You are. *(She tries to grab him)* I should kill you.

ALEX

(Holds her back.) Vicky, calm down.

JILL

(Enters) I hope I'm not interrupting anything.

BRIAN

(Cell rings, he answers it) Hello. Hi, how are you? *(BRIAN continues to adlib loudly as the scene goes on)*

ALEX

(Holding on to CLAIR) Fortunately yes. *(Beat)* Doctor, how is he doing?

JILL

Not well. *(CLAIR hugs ALEX and begins to cry, ALEX rubs her back. GREG begins to cry).*

GREG

(JOHN begins to move a little) Oh my gosh.

ALEX

What's wrong?

GREG

I just saw him move.

CLAIR

That's impossible, he's unconscious. *(JOHN starts to move some more)* Oh my goodness. *(Runs over to JOHN)* Aaron, can you hear me?

JOHN

Mom…

ALEX

(Runs over to CLAIR) Aaron, son, how are you feeling?

JOHN

Dad, is that you?

CLAIR

Yes, it's your mom and dad.

MARIA

(Frustrated, talking to actors) Guys stop for a second. *(Annoyed)* Brian!

BRIAN

(Talking on phone) Hold on. *(To MARIA)* What is it Maria, *(beat)* can't it wait? Don't you see me on the phone?

MARIA

Do you have to talk so loud? We're in the middle of the scene. Don't you think you should take that conversation out of the theater, where no one will be disturbed?

BRIAN

Oh, of course. Um…I'll just hang up. Hello, yeah, I'll call you back. What, oh yeah *(Starts laughing loudly, MARIA looks at him)*. I gotta go *(hangs up phone)*.

MARIA

Continue please.

JOHN

(He slowly opens his eyes). Mom, where am I?

CLAIR

You're in the hospital. You were unconscious, but you're going to be okay.

JILL

I'm going to need you guys to leave.

JOHN

No mommy, don't leave.

CLAIR

Its okay Aaron, we'll be here, we'll be right outside the door. *(blackout)*

MARIA

(Lights come back up) Good job guys. Let's take a small break. *(The actors exit)*

BRIAN

Thank God. I need one.

MARIA

You just got here. Besides I need to talk to you.

BRIAN

I'm sorry for being late. If you want, next time I'll bring you something from starbucks.

MARIA

That's okay. Besides, this is not about being late. We have a small problem, but I know how to fix it. I need you to operate the lights in the last scene of act two.

BRIAN

Why?

MARIA

Because there is no one else to do it. Normally one of the cast members would do it, whenever they are not on stage, but the whole cast is on stage during the last scene.

BRIAN

Why are the cast members operating the lighting board. I thought Michael was suppose to do that. I mean he is the lighting board operator, correct?

MARIA

Brian, where have you been? Michael quit two weeks ago.

BRIAN

(Shocked) WHAT? What do you mean he quit?

MARIA

He quit. He said he found a better paying job, so he quit.

BRIAN

But we weren't paying him.

MARIA

Exactly. He found a paying job in New York and said that he wouldn't have time for us. I thought I mentioned this to you.

BRIAN

I don't remember. You said two weeks ago, right? *(Pause, thinking)* Was I even here two weeks ago?

MARIA

It doesn't matter now. The whole point is, I need you to operate the board for the last scene. You think you can do it?

BRIAN

Well, sure. It's not a problem.

MARIA

Thank you. You're a life saver.

BRIAN

What flavor?

MARIA

What?

BRIAN

You get it. Life savor, what flavor? It was a joke.

MARIA

It wasn't funny. Okay cast, the break is over.

JILL

(Walks towards MARIA) May I talk to you really quickly.

MARIA

Sure. What's up?

JILL

Uh, can I speak to you in private.

MARIA

(To BRIAN) Um...could you please–

BRIAN

Oh, sure, that's not a problem. *(He takes his binder and stands it up to cover himself).*

MARIA

Brian, what are you doing?

BRIAN

I'm giving you privacy. Trust me this binder is tough; I can't hear a thing.

MARIA

Brian, go backstage. *(BRIAN exits to backstage).* What do you need to talk about?

JILL

Are you aware as the doctor I only have three lines?

MARIA

Yes, I read the play.

JILL

Well, I was wondering maybe, we could change that. Add a few lines so that the doctor seems more relevant. Right now, as the doctor I feel insignificant.

MARIA

Jill, I can't do that. This is a published script. I am not allowed to adapt it in any way. Unless I pay, which, I don't have the money for that.

JILL

What about a small monologue? It'll be about the conditions of Aaron. You won't even have to write it. I'll write it.

MARIA

No.

JILL

Maybe you could give me someone else's. For instant, in the scene Clair mentions it's impossible for Aaron to move, because he is unconscious. Don't you think I should be the one to say that. I am the doctor, don't you think a doctor would know that better than anyone else.

MARIA

Jill, I am not changing this play. Is that all you wanted to talk about?

JILL

You know, if you wouldn't have made the mistake in the first place and just cast me as Vicky, we wouldn't be having this talk.

MARIA

(Frustrated) Jill, I did not make a mistake. Clair is doing a great job as Vicky. Can we please just drop it?

JILL

The doctor. That's all you saw me as; a doctor with three lines.

MARIA

You're not just the doctor.

JILL

Oh, please, the stupid grandmother. The drunk grandmother. Thanks a lot. Don't you think I have much more talent than that?

MARIA

Yes you do. Your talent has nothing to do with your roles. Now can we please drop this subject. What's done is done. We can't change it now.

JILL

Yes we can. If you let me be Vicky and allow Clair to play my roles everything will be great. Besides, I know all her lines and her blocking.

MARIA

Jill. The answer is no. Go get ready for the next scene.

JILL

(Walks away) I'm not in the next scene.

MARIA

Go get ready to operate the lighting board. *(JILL exits)*

CLAIR

(Enters frantically) Maria, I need to leave, now!

MARIA

Why? What's wrong?

CLAIR

My sister just called me. She's in labor. I have to go see about her.

MARIA

Well, is everything okay?

CLAIR

Not really? Her husband is stuck in traffic, she can't reach a phone, and no one is home. I have to go and take her to the hospital.

MARIA

What do you mean she can't reach a phone, she called you. And why didn't she call 911?

CLAIR

I don't know. I gotta go.

MARIA

You can't *(CLAIR slams door as she exits)* –go.

BRIAN

(Enters) Are you finished with your private meeting?

MARIA

Yes. Unfortunately, we might have to cancel the rest of the rehearsal.

BRIAN

Oh, how sad. *(Gets his belongings)* Well, I guess I'll see you tomorrow.

MARIA

Where are you going?

BRIAN

Home. You just said rehearsal is cancelled. *(Yells)* Everyone rehearsal is cancelled for the rest of the night.

MARIA

Brian, I did not say that.

GREG

(GREG, ALEX, JOHN, SARAH, and JILL enters with belongings) What's going on?

BRIAN

Maria is allowing us to go home early.

JOHN

(To MARIA) Is that true.

MARIA

Brian, that's not–

BRIAN

That's what she said.

MARIA

I said I might have to–

BRIAN

See you guys tomorrow *(exits)*.

MARIA

Forget him. Guys I need you to–

GREG

Buy Maria, see you tomorrow (*ALEX, JOHN, SARAH,* and *JILL say bye to MARIA, they all exit*).

MARIA

Don't *(door slams)* leave. *(Blackout)*.

ACT ONE SCENE TWO

This scene takes place the next day June 21.

MARIA

(Lights come up. MARIA, GREG, JOHN, JILL, ALEX, and SARAH are sitting around awaiting. BRIAN enters). You're late, again. *(Beat)* Guys go get ready for the next scene *(GREG, JOHN, JILL, ALEX, and SARAH exit).*

BRIAN

I'm aware. I have a watch *(Sits next to Maria).*

MARIA

Are you aware, that we have been waiting for you. *(Looks at watch)* You're thirty minutes late. We wasted thirty minutes. *(Beat)* What's your excuse this time?

BRIAN

I was at home watching Arthur.

MARIA

You can't be serious.

BRIAN

(Seriously) I'm very serious. I love watching Arthur, it's very educational.

MARIA

Brian, I thought I told you to be on time last night.

BRIAN

Well, you're thinking right, because you did.

MARIA

So, why are you late?

BRIAN

I thought I explained that already?

MARIA

Arthur is not an excuse. It's not a reason to be late to rehearsal. You must be here on time. I don't know how clear I can make that. No more being late Brian. *(Beat)* Now, get your script, I need you to read lines for Clair.

BRIAN

Do what for what?

MARIA

I need you to read Clair's lines for the rehearsal.

BRIAN

Why. What's wrong with Clair?

MARIA

She left early yesterday, because her sister went into labor. She took her to the hospital.

BRIAN

That's amazing, I didn't even know that Clair had a sister.

MARIA

She called me today, and said she can't make rehearsal. Her sister, nor the baby is doing well. So, we'll just have to do the rehearsal without her.

BRIAN

We can't rehearse without her. Why don't we just call it a night.

MARIA

What? No, we are not doing that, just read her lines.

BRIAN

I still say we just call it a night.

MARIA

I can't do that. This show opens this week. I don't have time to cancel rehearsals.

BRIAN

It's just one day.

MARIA

It will be two if you can't yesterday.

BRIAN

That was your fault. You shouldn't have cancelled it.

MARIA

I didn't cancel– ...Brian would you please just–

BRIAN

Do I really have to?

MARIA

(Annoyed) Get a script and read her lines.

BRIAN

Well, you don't have to yell about it.

MARIA

I WASN'T YELLING!

BRIAN

Well, you are now. *(She sighs heavily at him)* I'm getting the script *(Gets his script from book bag)*.

MARIA

Guys, please get in place for this scene. Thank you. *(The actors except JOHN get into place)*.

BRIAN

Do the actors know about Clair. I mean they know I'm reading, right?

MARIA

Yes they do. I told them within the thirty minutes you weren't here.

BRIAN

Oh. Well, you didn't have to say it like that. *(Opens script)* What page?

MARIA

Twenty-three.

BRIAN

JOHN enters and lies on the bed; a brief black out occurs then the lights slowly fade in. Brian clears throat). Remember when I used to read to you at night, before you went to bed? *(JOHN nods head yes)*. You mind if I read to you? *(To MARIA)* What book is Clair reading to him?

MARIA

That doesn't matter at this point?

BRIAN

Oh, sorry.

MARIA

Start from the beginning please.

BRIAN

(BRIAN clears throat). Remember when I used to read to you at night, before you went to bed? *(JOHN nods head yes).* You mind if I read to you?

JOHN

I would love that. It'll bring–

BRIAN

(To MARIA) Are you sure it doesn't matter. The script says that she reads *The Three Little Pigs.*

MARIA

There is note in the back of the script that says it's okay if the director decides to use another book. Now, can you please just continue? *(BRIAN nods yes)* John, start your line again.

JOHN

I would love that. It'll bring back sweet memories.

BRIAN

(GREG enters) Not you again, get out, and don't come back.

JOHN

(GREG intends to leave) No, don't leave. Mom, I want to talk to him.

BRIAN

Aaron, he is bad news. I don't want you around people like him.

JOHN

Mom, please I must speak with him. *(There is complete silence for about 5 seconds. After the pause they both recite each other's name).* I'm sorry you go first.

GREG

No, no, you; tell me what you need to tell me.

JOHN

Jason, please you go first, I can wait. *(GREG folds his arms as if in protest to speak first).* Alright, I'll go first. I'm sorry I ruined your party.

GREG

Are you crazy? You didn't ruin it. I'm sorry I gave you all that stuff. I didn't know it was going to make you...I'm sorry.

JOHN

Come up here. *(GREG gets on top of the bed).*

BRIAN

Is he really suppose to jump on the bed? It looks...stupid. It doesn't look right. Besides I don't think the bed could actually hold that much weight.

MARIA

Brian, the bed is fine, and keep your negative comments to yourself.

BRIAN

All I was saying is that–

MARIA

Brian. Be quiet. John, continue please.

JOHN

I know you think this is your fault. You know, my mother thinks it's her fault. This is no one's fault but, mine. I made the decision to take ecstasy and drink beer. I was the one who did not use discretion. It is my fault. So, please, stop blaming yourself, *(brief silence, and blackout)*.

MARIA

(Light comes up over MARIA and BRIAN. BRIAN is reading a magazine.) Great, let's go on to the next scene. *(To BRIAN)* When reading for Clair, just read. That's it. *(Lights out over MARIA and BRIAN).*

SARAH

(Lights come up over stage, SARAH and the party extras are on stage, they party for a brief moment before GREG enters, SARAH notices him). Hey stranger, long time no see. Where have you been?

GREG

I went to visit Aaron.

SARAH

How's the slugger doing?

GREG

He's doing. *(Beat)* Uh…Lizzie I need to talk to you alone.

SARAH

Jason, we're partying, come on, party with us. We can talk later.

GREG

No. I want to talk now. *(GREG talks to the party extras).* Excuse me; may I have your attention? *(The party and music stops).* The party's over; everyone please leave. *(The party people adlib disapproval)* Come on, get out. *(They begin to leave).*

SARAH

(Pulling him aside) What is wrong with you? You're ruining a good thing. *(Talking to the party people)* Guys, you don't have to leave.

GREG

Yes you do. Everyone out *(beat)* now.

SARAH

(Party extras exit). What is wrong with you? You never turn down a party.

GREG

I'm changing, Lizzie...I've changed. I can't do this anymore.

SARAH

You can't do what anymore; what are you talking about?

GREG

I can't live this lifestyle. No more parties, drugs, or alcohol, it ruins lives. It makes people unconscious and—

SARAH

Are you still worried about Aaron? Get over it. Aaron is fine. Besides, he was a punk; he took too much too soon. You're a pro; you can keep partying without passing out.

GREG

Lizzie, I don't wanna do this anymore. I'm done with it, and you should be done with it too.

SARAH

If you're gonna punk out on me, then we can't be friends.

GREG

That is not a problem with me; you know where the door is. *(SARAH exits, blackout).*

MARIA

(GREG exits, the scene is being set for the JOHNSON's house). A spotlight appears on MARIA) Let's keep it moving guys, thank you. *(JILL enters with belongings ready to leave)* You're not leaving, are you?

JILL

Yes. I'll see you tomorrow.

MARIA

Wait a minute. *(Stands)* Where are you going?

JILL

I have a manicure appointment.

MARIA

We have a rehearsal to do.

JILL

Maria, I need to leave now, or I will be late. I cannot be late. My nails cannot be late.

MARIA

Jill, you can't be serious. Can't you cancel the appointment or postpone it?

JILL

(Shocked) Cancel, postpone, how dare you?

MARIA

What? What did I say?

JILL

I cannot postpone my nails. My nails need care. How dare you suggest I cancel or postpone. I have to get my nails done, and that's final

MARIA

Jill, please, we need you in order to rehearse. *(Announcing)* The show opens *this week.* Are we all aware of that?

JILL

Have Brian read my lines.

MARIA

He's reading for Clair.

JILL

Then you read it. I'm getting my nails done, now.

MARIA

Jill, you can't leave *(JILL walks towards exit)* Jill, please don't leave *(JILL exits)*. I don't believe this. *(To BRIAN)* Why didn't you say anything.

BRIAN

What did you want me to say?

MARIA

You could have told her, she couldn't go.

BRIAN

I thought to, but–

MARIA

You didn't want to argue?

BRIAN

No.

MARIA

You realize she already made up her mind?

BRIAN

No.

MARIA

You thought she wasn't going to listen to you?

BRIAN

No, I was reading and I didn't want to lose my place.

MARIA

(Sighs hard; speaking to BRIAN) I'M going backstage to meditate. We will continue rehearsal in an hour.

BRIAN

Maybe we should just go home.

MARIA

(Looks at watch) It's only seven. We still have three more hours of rehearsal. We'll all take an hour break, and I'll call Jill and Clair and hopefully they'll be able to come and rehearse.

BRIAN

It'll be too late by then.

MARIA

I need as many rehearsals as I can get. Don't argue with me. I just don't understand, does anyone care about this production besides me. Does anyone care about the kids?

BRIAN

What kids?

MARIA

The kids from Make-A-Wish Foundation.

BRIAN

What do they have to do with anything?

MARIA

(Frustrated) Tell the cast they get an hour break. Rehearsal resumes at 8PM *(exits)*.

BRIAN

(Yells) Cast and crew, please come to the stage! *(GREG, JOHN, ALEX, SARAH and extras enter).* Jill had to leave, so Maria thinks it's best if we take an hour break and then resume with rehearsal. She's going to call Jill and Clair later and hopefully they can make it back here in time.

SARAH

But, that doesn't make sense. It'll probably be to late by then.

BRIAN

I know, I told Maria that already, but she has spoken. You have an hour for break. *(Puts coat on, and gathers belongings)* If Maria asks, tell her I went to Starbucks *(exits)*.

GREG

I'll be napping backstage *(exits)*.

SARAH

This is stupid. What are we supposed to do for an hour?

JOHN

We can have sex.

SARAH

Shut up John.

JOHN

Come on Sarah. You know you want me.

SARAH

Keep dreaming.

JOHN

I will. They'll be sexy and wet.

SARAH

Oh, gosh, you're so disgusting.

JOHN

You know you like it.

SARAH

What makes you think I like you? You're not even my type.

JOHN

What is your type?

SARAH

Well, for starters, someone who can drink legally.

JOHN

Age ain't nuttin' but a number.

SARAH

It would never work. Older women can't date younger men.

JOHN

That's not true. Halle is older than Erik.

SARAH

You saw how their relationship ended up.

JOHN

Not all relationships end badly. How about Demi and Ashton? They love each other.

SARAH

It's nothing more than a physical attraction. I need more than that.

JOHN

Are you saying, I'm sexy.

SARAH

John, you need help.

JOHN

Than help me. Help me, baby. Give me the help I need.

SARAH

Only a licensed doctor could do that.

JOHN

What's that suppose to mean? You act like I have problems or something.

SARAH

You do.

JOHN

What's my problem?

SARAH

Which one?

JOHN

Sarah, you don't mean that, do you? *(Pause)* Well, what's my problems, name three.

SARAH

Well, for starters, you're way to young for me. Second, I hate the way you wear your hair, it's so out of fashion. Third, you think you're God's gift to women, I hate it when men think like that, you're pushy, immature, vulgar, you have a disgusting mind, you don't know how to act like a gentleman, and I hate it when you–

JOHN

Alright, I get it. I said name three. Goodness, next time just say you hate me *(Hangs head)* .

SARAH

John, I don't hate you, I hate some things about you, but I don't hate you.

JOHN

(Lifts head, smiles) Oh. That's good. Well, I will change the way I act, so that you can like me better.

SARAH

John, you don't have to change for me.

JOHN

But I want to. It'll be my pleasure. Would you like to go out with me.

SARAH

Are you crazy, a date? No way.

JOHN

Not a date. We can walk to a restaurant around the area.

SARAH

I don't know about that.

JOHN

Why not? We have a whole hour to kill. Why not kill it together?

SARAH

Because then I would be your accomplice, and I don't look good in an orange jumpsuit.

JOHN

I'm serious Sarah, just as friends. *(He puts his arm out, she puts her arm around his).*

SARAH

Don't you think we should get our coats before leaving?

JOHN

Of Course. I'll escort you to the backstage area.

SARAH

(They exit backstage) So where are we going to eat? *(Blackout)*

ACT ONE SCENE THREE

The next day, Wednesday June 22. MARIA, CLAIR, JILL, SARAH, JOHN, ALEX, and GREG are sitting in the audience area.

CLAIR

So after receiving the speeding ticket, I dash off to my sister's house. My sister was in there screaming. As I go to open the door, it's locked, and I didn't have a key. Finally, I got enough sense to call the cops on my cell. They broke in and got her. It was so bad that they had to deliver the baby in the house. The next day the doctor said there were problems. I panicked. *(Speaking to MARIA)* That's when I called you, and said I wasn't coming. After a couple of hours the doctor came back, and said everything was okay. I was so happy. Can you believe it? This is the third day of my life that I am an aunt.

JILL

What did they name the baby?

CLAIR

Jonathan Richard.

JOHN

Jonathan? What a great name. It's such a distinguished name. *(Sarah clears her throat),* but yet so common.

MARIA

Well, I'm glad everything went well.

JILL

Does anyone want to hear how my manicure appointment went.

MARIA

No, thank you. We need to start this rehearsal. We'll have to start without Brian, again.

SARAH

Well, who's going to operate the lighting board.

MARIA

We'll have to do this scene without the lights. We can't wait any longer. After we're done with this scene we will do Clair's scene that she missed yesterday, then we will begin from the beginning. *(MARIA sits at directors table, GREG, JILL, SARAH, CLAIR, ALEX, and JOHN get ready for the scene).* Lights.

JOHN

(GREG, JILL, SARAH, AND EXTRAS enter. ALEX, CLAIR and JOHN enter. When they enter everyone on stage yells "Surprise!"). Oh, my goodness, this is wonderful. *(He hugs ALEX and then CLAIR)* THANKS dad, thanks mom, you have made me so happy. I want to thank all of you for coming. Most of all I want to thank you all for the love and support you showed me while I was in the hospital. I made some stupid choices and I had to pay the consequences. I just thank God that I'm still alive. Thanks again.
(Everyone cheers, and returns to partying (drinking, dancing, conversing)).

UNCLE JACOB

(CLAIR and ALEX walk toward the guest to thank and welcome them. UNCLE JACOB and SARAH walk towards JOHN. JACOB gives JOHN a rough hug)
Hey, there's my nephew.

JOHN

Uncle Jake.

UNCLE JACOB

How are you doing, buddy, you keeping out of trouble?

JOHN

Yes, I am doing the best I can.

SARAH

(Hugs JOHN) How are you Aaron, you feeling well *(JOHN nods yes)*? That's good.

UNCLE JACOB

(Tries to wrestle with JOHN) Of course, he's okay. He's, my slugger.

SARAH

Jake, calm down.

UNCLE JACOB

Gloria, don't tell me what to do.

SARAH

Well, if you weren't acting like a child I wouldn't have to.

UNCLE JACOB

What is your problem?

SARAH

There is nothing wrong with me, however, your problem is too much beer. *(Beat)* Slow down before you hurt yourself. *(UNCLE JACOB and SARAH walk away arguing).*

JOHN

(GREG walks towards JOHN. JOHN sees him and smiles. He puts his hand towards GREG and they shake hands). Hey, thanks for coming.

GREG

When your mom called me I thought she was plotting my death *(They both laugh)*.

JOHN

She was very upset, however, after I talked to her, she realize you weren't all that bad. *(Changing the subject)* So, how's Lizzie and the rest of the crew.

GREG

I don't know, *(beat)* I don't hang out with them anymore. I changed, after I saw you in the hospital, I had to stop.

JOHN

That's good. I'm happy for you.

GREG

I'm happy for you too. To see you alive is a good feeling. *(Pause)* I'm sorry—

JOHN

Don't apologize; *(pause)* it's good seeing you again *(he puts his hands toward GREG and they shake, then they hug.*

CLAIR

(CLAIR and JILL walk towards JOHN). Aaron, look who is here.

JOHN

(He looks and smiles, he walks to JILL and hugs her) Grandma Rose thanks for coming. You didn't have to travel so far for me.

JILL

I know, but you're worth it, you're my puff cakes. How are you doing, puff cakes?

JOHN

I'm doing much better, now that I know you're here.

JILL

Ain't he sweet *(takes a dollar out of her purse)* here you go puff cakes, don't spend it all on one place. *(Walking away with CLAIR and speaking to her)* What do you have to drink?

CLAIR

We have juice, water, soda—

JILL

Do you have any liquor?

JOHN

(Talking to GREG, referring to dollar) This may not look like a lot, but the last time I saw her she gave me quarter *(They laugh)*.

GREG

That's funny. *(Beat)* Explain something to me.

JOHN

What?

GREG

Puff cakes?

JOHN

(Laughing) When I was a baby, I had big puffy cheeks *(beat)* she's been calling me that ever since then.

ALEX

(Banging fork against glass, to get everyone's attention) May I have everyone's attention? I want to make a toast to the best son a father could have. *(Everyone has a drink already, JILL brings a glass to AARON, and CLAIR brings one to GREG).* Although he made his mistakes, he still is a son that makes me very proud. If I had a choice, I wouldn't want any other young gentleman as my son. He's the best son ever, *(he raises his glass)* cheers *(Everyone cheers and toast each other and drink)*.

MARIA

And this is where the music comes in and the lights fade out. Good job, guys. We're going to take a ten-minute break, and then we'll start with Clair's scene. I'll be back stage meditating *(exits)*.

JILL

(GREG, ALEX and extras exit). So, what are we supposed to do for ten minutes. That's hardly enough time to do anything.

JOHN

Why don't you get a pedicure to go with your manicure.

JILL

Shut up John. I swear you're so immature.

SARAH

(To JOHN) See, I told you.

JOHN

(To SARAH) Maybe we can go on another date.

SARAH

It wasn't a date. I thought you were trying to change.

JILL

Change, why would he change?

CLAIR

Who would he change for?

JOHN

Sarah. She said, if I change to her liking, she would date me. Maybe even have sex.

SARAH

You see what I mean. You're a disgusting pig. You can change all you want, I would never date you.

JILL

You said you would date him?

SARAH

No I did not. He's dreaming again.

JOHN

Wet and wild baby, wet and wild.

CLAIR

You're so disgusting, John. When are you gonna grow up?

JOHN

Why do you care? Are you waiting for me to grow up, so you can date me?

CLAIR

John, keep dreaming. That's the only date you'll ever have. I swear he's so annoying.

ALEX

(JILL, *and* SARAH *adlib agreement with* CLAIR. CLAIR, JILL, *and* SARAH *exit.* ALEX, *and* GREG *enter*) What's going on?

JOHN

Nothing. Just having fun with the girls.

GREG

What kind of fun?

JOHN

They all have crushes on me. I'm just trying to make their wishes come true.

GREG

In your dreams buddy.

ALEX

We heard everything. If you wanna girl to like you, you have to stop being so adolescent. Those are women, not girls. They graduated high school already. They don't want to deal with high school boys.

JOHN

It doesn't matter, I'm too young for them.

GREG

Age is nothing, but a number. Women don't care about age, they care about personality. You can be forty-five, but if you're acting like a teenager hitting puberty, she wants nothing to do with you.

ALEX

It's all about maturity. A woman wants someone she can talk to like an adult. A man who can understand her.

MARIA

(Enters). We will now resume with our rehearsal.

ALEX

Was that ten minutes?

MARIA

I don't know. All I know is that I am relaxed and ready to continue. I am so relaxed that nothing can get me unrelaxed, or upset. Now let's begin.

BRIAN

(Enters) Hello everyone.

MARIA

(Unrelaxed) You're late. Do you realize how late you are? Why can't you show up on time? Is it against your religion to be on time?

BRIAN

Are you okay? I'm sorry I'm late.

MARIA

What is it now, Starbucks, Arthur?

BRIAN

No. I was playing video games and lost track of time. I would have called you but–

MARIA

Let me guess, you didn't feel like it.

BRIAN

No. I couldn't find your phone number.

MARIA

My phone number is listed in the cast and crew directory. Everyone got one.

BRIAN

I know. I got one too.

MARIA

Than why didn't you use it?

BRIAN

Because I misplaced it, and I didn't feel like looking for it. It's not a big deal, I'm here, right?

MARIA

(Takes a deep breath) Right. *(To GREG, ALEX, and JOHN)* Guys, go get ready, thank you. We're about to start, we just finished a ten-minute break, before that we finished the last scene of act two.

BRIAN

Who did the lights for me?

MARIA

No one. We had to do the scene without the lights.

BRIAN

Oh, okay. *(JOHN and CLAIR enter, JOHN lies on bed, CLAIR sits on chair next to the bed)* Oh, hey Clair. How are you doing? Did your sister have the baby?

CLAIR

Yes. She had a boy.

BRIAN

Oh, that's so sweet. Maria, did you hear that, her sister had a boy.

MARIA

I know. Clair told us before we began rehearsal. It was probably around the time you were playing video games. Clair start when you're ready.

CLAIR

Remember when I used to read to you at night, before you went to bed? *(JOHN nods head yes. CLAIR shows JOHN a book).* You mind if I read to you?

JOHN

I would love that. It'll bring back sweet memories.

CLAIR

(Opens children's book), and reads. As she reads GREG enters. As she is reading JOHN looks up at GREG, after glancing at JOHN she turns around and sees GREG, GREG becomes frightened). Not you again, get out, and don't come back.

JOHN

(GREG intends to leave) No, don't leave. Mom, I want to talk to him.

CLAIR

Aaron, he is bad news. I don't want you around people like him.

JOHN

Mom, please I must speak with him. *(CLAIR shakes her head yes as a hesitant approval; she exits. GREG sits down next to JOHN. There is complete silence for about 5 seconds. After the pause they both recite each other's name).* I'm sorry you go first.

GREG

No, no, you; tell me what you need to tell me.

JOHN

Jason, please you go first, I can wait. *(GREG folds his arms as if in protest to speak first).* Alright, I'll go first. I'm sorry I ruined your party.

GREG

Are you crazy? You didn't ruin it. I'm sorry I gave you all that stuff. I didn't know it was going to make you…I'm sorry.

JOHN

Come up here. *(As GREG sits on the bed).* I know you think this is your fault my mom thinks it's her fault. This is no one's fault but, mine. I made the decision to take ecstasy and drink beer. I was the one who did not use discretion. It is my fault. So, please, stop blaming yourself, *(brief silence, and blackout).*

MARIA

(Lights come up) Guys, that was good. Please set the stage for the opening scene, thank you.

CLAIR

(Concerned) Maria, there's a mouse whole backstage.

MARIA

A mouse whole? It's probably just a regular hole, I'm sure it's not a mouse hole, so don't worry about it.

CLAIR

I don't know, it looks just like a mouse hole. I've see one before.

MARIA

Brian, can you go backstage with Clair to see what she is talking about?

BRIAN

(He's playing a video game on his phone) Not now, I'm on level sixteen, I've never gotten this far.

MARIA

Greg, John can you guys go–

JOHN

Sure thing, it's not a problem.

MARIA

(GREG, JOHN, and CLAIR exit). Brian *(No response)*, Brian *(No response, Maria takes his phone)* Brian!

BRIAN

Maria! *(Takes phone back)* Oh, man! I died; you made me die.

MARIA

Do you have to play that now. We're in the middle of a rehearsal. You really need to go backstage and see what Clair is talking about.

BRIAN

Why, what's backstage?

MARIA

She claims there's a mouse hole back there. You need to go check it out.

BRIAN

Trust me there is no mouse hole backstage *(CLAIR screams)* What was that?

CLAIR

(Frantically enters) I saw him, I saw him!

MARIA

Saw who. Who's back there?

CLAIR

There's a mouse.

MARIA

Oh, no. Why does this have to happen.

JILL

(JILL, ALEX, and SARAH enter) What's going on?

CLAIR

There's a mouse backstage.

JOHN

(JOHN and GREG enters) It's gonna be hard to catch that thing. He can run.

MARIA

What happened

GREG

(Referring to JOHN) Genius, over here takes a broom and sticks it in the whole

JOHN

It's what I'm good for.

SARAH

Shut up! Gosh, you're so disgusting.

GREG

Obviously, the mouse got scared and ran. He's somewhere backstage. You're gonna need an exterminator.

MARIA

I don't have the funds for that. This can't be happening. Brian, you need to figure something out.

BRIAN

Why me. I'm not the one who let it loose.

MARIA

Brian, please.

BRIAN

What do you want me to do?

MARIA

I don't know. Get a mouse trap or something. Just figure it out. Guys let's continue this rehearsal.

CLAIR

Well, I don't wanna go back there with that thing still running around.

JILL

Exactly. I refuse to share the backstage with that filthy beast.

JOHN

It's just a mouse.

MARIA

Guys, it won't hurt you. It's more afraid of you than you are of it.

JILL

It might have rabies.

MARIA

It doesn't have–

SARAH

She has a point *(Everyone adlibs in agreement)*.

MARIA

Fine. I'll cancel rehearsal, again. But please be here tomorrow, on time *(Blackout)*.

ACT TWO

ACT TWO SCENE ONE

This scene takes place on June 23. Night before show opens.

ALEX

(Banging fork against glass, to get everyone's attention) May I have everyone's attention? I want to make a toast to the best son a father could have. *(Everyone has a drink already, Jill brings a glass to Aaron, and Clair brings one to Greg).* Although he made his mistakes, he still is a son that makes me very proud. If I had a choice, I wouldn't want any other young gentleman as my son. He's the best son ever, *(he raises his glass)* cheers *(Everyone cheers and toast each other and drink. The background music gets louder and everyone dances, the light goes out slowly. When the lights come up the actors do curtain calls; after curtain calls a black out occurs and the actors exit the stage; the lights come up).*

MARIA

(Gives standing ovation, crying) That was beautiful. That was the most beautiful performance I have ever seen. I loved it. I loved it. *(To BRIAN)* Wasn't the at beautiful? It was beautiful. Guys you have made me proud. Go clean up backstage, and then come back out here for notes *(Cast exits).* Plus I have a surprise. *(Sits)* That was beautiful.

BRIAN

Are you okay?

MARIA

Yeah, I'm fine. Thanks for taking care of the mouse problem. I knew I could count on you.

BRIAN

It was no problem. Are you sure you're okay?

MARIA

Yes, I'm fine. So, how did you take care of the problem?

BRIAN

I brought some mouse traps and put them backstage.

MARIA

How many, and where did you put them?

BRIAN

I don't know about ten or fifteen. I put them in corners, by holes, wherever I thought a mouse would go.

MARIA

It won't be a problem, right? I mean the cast will be able to see the mouse traps?

BRIAN

Yeah, it won't be a problem.

MARIA

I hope not. I don't want the cast stepping in them by mistake.

BRIAN

Don't worry.

MARIA

(Cast enters with belongings, applauding them) There they are. You were beautiful. Gather 'round, I have something to tell you. Have you guys ever heard of Artsy Magazine?

JOHN

Of course.

JILL

It's the best Art magazine in the world. Everyone who is famous today, is famous because of that magazine.

MARIA

Well, Anthony Bridges is coming here–

CLAIR

Anthony Bridges!

MARIA

Yeah, do you know him?

JILL

What do you mean; everyone knows him. He's the best writer for that magazine. He's coming here?

MARIA

Well, yeah. He's coming to review the play.

ALEX

That's amazing. How did you get him to do that?

MARIA

I wrote the magazine, and they sent him? Wow! Is he that famous?

GREG

Are you crazy? You don't know who he is? If he reviews this play, we have a big chance of becoming famous.

JILL

Well, that sucks. He only talks about the leads of a show. He won't even notice me.

CLAIR

I'm finally going to be discovered. *(Everyone adlibs)*

MARIA

Guys, please may I have your attention. That's all fine and dandy, but don't forget the purpose. I called the magazine so they can interview me, so that I could tell them about the Make-A-Wish Foundation. The whole purpose of this company is for the fund-raiser. Don't forget, guys. This show is for the kids, it's not about ourselves.

CLAIR

You're right. I'm sorry I got all cocky.

MARIA

It's okay, just make sure you guys remember that. You guys go home and get some rest. Tomorrow is our last rehearsal...the only time you get to mess up. *(Looks at Brian)* The last time you can show up late. It's the last time–

CLAIR

Maria.

MARIA

Yes, Clair.

CLAIR

I think you're mistaken. Tonight was our last rehearsal. Tomorrow is opening night.

MARIA

You can't be serious.

SARAH

You forgot? That's so unlike you.

MARIA

(Panicking) Is it really tomorrow night. It can't be. We're not ready.

GREG

I think we're ready.

MARIA

But we haven't rehearsed all the way through without stopping. We can't. We just can't.

BRIAN

Maria, they're fine. Everything will be fine. Just calm down.

MARIA

Are you guys sure you're okay?

ALEX

We're fine. Aren't we? *(Everyone adlibs in agreement)*

MARIA

(Worried) Well, if you say so. I've never done a performance without a tech rehearsal. *(Thinking)* I don't think we should do this. We should probably cancel.

BRIAN

Stop all that foolishness. Everything will be perfectly fine *(Blackout)*.

ACT TWO SCENE TWO

USHER

(When the lights come up the stage is set for the rave scene; MARIA, VIOLA STEPHANIE, and ANTHONY BRIDGES are sitting in the audience (lights are focused on the audience area). The usher is standing. A man enters). Hello, welcome to Jenkins Theater, may I help you to your seat?

MAN

No thanks I can find it *(he walks towards the seats and looks for his seat).*

WOMAN

(A woman enters with a bag of chips and soda bottle; speaking to USHER). Excuse me, do you know where I can get tickets at?

USHER

Yes, at the box office.

WOMAN

Where's that at?

USHER

(Sarcastically) Gee, I'm not sure, maybe outside where the big ass sign Box office is.

WOMAN

(Shocked) Well, you don't have to be so rude.

USHER

Well, you don't have to be so dumb. By the way, when you plan to come in here, know that you can't bring in food or drinks.

WOMAN

Are you serious?

USHER

(Sarcastically) No, I'm joking with you, *(beat)* of course I'm serious stupid. Didn't you see the sign at the concessions stand and the theater door.

WOMAN

(Shocked) No, I guess I overlooked it.

USHER

Whatever, no food or drink in the theater *(MAN is still looking for his seat)*.

WOMAN

I won't eat it I promise.

USHER

Then don't it eat in the lobby *(pushes her out the door)* thank you.

MAN

(Man walks over to the usher) Excuse me, would one of you help me with my seats?

USHER

I aught to slap you in your face. Just a minute ago I offered to help you and you said, *(mocking him)* no I can find it. If you weren't so stubborn, and trying to be Mr Don't need help from an usher, you wouldn't have this problem now.

MAN

Can you just help me?

USHER

(He snatches the ticket from the man) Give me the ticket *(walks man to his seat)*

BRIAN

(Walks towards Maria). Hey, what's up? *(Sits next to her)*

MARIA

Nothing. What's wrong?

BRIAN

There's nothing wrong.

MARIA

Then why aren't you backstage?

BRIAN

I'm going to watch the play.

MARIA

Brian, I told you I needed you to operate the light board.

BRIAN

Yeah, I know, but that's not until act two. I'll go backstage during intermission.

MARIA

Brian, you should really be backstage, waiting until it's your turns to operate the light board. If anything you should probably operate it during the whole show.

BRIAN

No I shouldn't. I'm the stage manager, not the light board operator. You should be glad I agreed to operate it to begin with. *(BRIAN and MARIA argue; USHER sits WOMAN behind BRIAN, the lights fade out; WOMAN shushes the two).* Who the hell you shushing?

GREG

(A brief blackout occurs; the actors get into place. This scene begins at a rave party. GREG, JOHN, SARAH, and extras are on the stage. The scene opens with rave music. When lights come up all actors are dancing and "raving." Speaking to JOHN) Hey Aaron, isn't this party great. *(JOHN nods, pauses, then collapses. Everyone rushes over and panics)* Aaron, what's wrong? *(Kneels down and listens to JOHN's heart)* Oh my gosh he's not breathing. *The crowd goes silent).* Someone call 911.

SARAH

(SARAH takes her cellular phone and dials). Hello, my name is Liz—Lesley Higgins and I have a problem. There's this kid and he's not breathing. *(Pause)* I don't know how he stopped breathing; I just know he's not breathing. *(Pause)* Who cares about all of that, just get someone here fast. *(Pause)* We're by the old warehouse on Morris Drive; please hurry.

GREG

(He asks one of the party extras to watch over him (JOHN); then he walks towards SARAH) Why did you lie about your name?

SARAH

If the police find out what he was doing, there's a big chance we're all gonna get in trouble. I can't get in trouble; it would hurt me and my families' name.

GREG

So you rather worry about your reputation than someone else's life?

SARAH

What do you care, just make sure he doesn't die.

GREG

Well, the police should be here any minute

SARAH

Well, I'm leaving.

GREG

Where are you going?

SARAH

I don't want to be here when the cops arrive. I'll see you tomorrow by Lakeland Ave, that's where Houston's rave is; and Jason, don't bring the chump *(exits)*.

GREG

Lizzie, you can't leave me here *(police sirens are heard; the rave extra's disperse.* GREG *kneels down to* JOHN*)*. I'm sorry buddy. *(Blackout)*

MARIA

(Talking to Brian) Thank God, that went well. We're doing good, we're doing good.

(When the lights come up CLAIR enters. She looks over at JOHN and starts to cry; she walks toward JOHN) Aaron. Aaron, please speak to me. How could you do this to yourself? Why were you hanging around that crowd?
(Pause; sits next to JOHN and embraces him) Aaron, please don't die.

ALEX

(CLAIR weeps, ALEX enters and sees CLAIR, and he puts his head down, takes a deep breath and walks towards CLAIR). Honey *(CLAIR runs towards ALEX and they embrace)* Vicky, the doctor said he'll be okay.

CLAIR

(She let goes of ALEX.) We don't know that. Look at him. Robert look at him *(ALEX looks at him).* Does that look like he's going to be okay?

ALEX

Looks can be deceiving. Many people make miraculous recoveries.

CLAIR

This is our fault. We should have been stricter.

ALEX

Honey, don't start putting blame on anyone. No one could have prepared for anything like this. The only thing we can do now is to wait and pray. *(Blackout)*

MARIA

We're doing really good. This is the best day of my life.

BRIAN

(When the lights come up Alex is seen putting the "couch" together. He pauses, then runs off; speaking to Maria) You were saying?

GREG

(Goes to sit on the "couch", as he does so, he misses a chair and falls through the sheet, he gets up and tries to fix it, then sits) I can't believe he just collapsed. I feel bad; I could have killed him.

SARAH

Jason, none of this is your fault. Aaron chose to take X, and drink all that beer. No one forced him.

GREG

But, I suggested he take it to get comfortable. If I didn't suggest it, he wouldn't have taken it.

SARAH

Well, what's done is done. Don't go beating yourself up for what someone else did to themselves.

GREG

Lizzie. We have to stop doing this. This was a sign. Can't you see? If it happened to him, it could happen to us.

SARAH

Greg, don't go soft on me. *(Picks up a beer from the bar)* Come on, suck it up *(hands him the beer)* have a beer *(A camera flash is seen from the audience)*.

GREG

No. *(Stands up)* I need to go for a walk to clear my head. *(He exits the stage; blackout)*

USHER

(A light comes up by the audience. USHER walks towards WOMAN) Excuse me, ma'am, you can't take pictures in this theater.

WOMAN

Oh, I'm sorry.

GREG

(Lights go down in audience area, Lights come up on stage area. JOHN is lying on the bed and GREG is sitting on a chair besides him. GREG is crying). This is my fault. Why, did I suggest you take those pills?

CLAIR

(CLAIR and ALEX enter. They both look at GREG strangely). Who are you? How do you know my son?

GREG

(He looks up at them) Oh, you're his parents? My name is Jason. I'm his friend; we hang out a lot.

CLAIR

(Angry) Are you one of the friends who got him in this state?

GREG

(Hesitant) I...I'm not sure what—

CLAIR

You are. *(She tries to grab him)* I should kill you.

ALEX

(Holds her back.) Vicky, calm down.

JILL

(Enters with a tape recorder, places it on the table next to the bed. Everyone on stage look confused. Under her doctor's coat is another costume one can barely see.) I hope I'm not interrupting anything.

ALEX

(Holding on to CLAIR) Fortunately yes. *(Beat)* Doctor, how is he doing?

JILL

He's not doing well *(CLAIR hugs ALEX and begins to cry, ALEX rubs her back. GREG begins to cry)*, but you know, I'm not just a doctor. *(She pushes a button on the recorder. The music comes on. Jill sings and dance with full costume. When she's done, she returns to the scene as if nothing happened. See page 211 for the song she sings).*

GREG

(Shocked; he continues) Oh my gosh.

ALEX

What's wrong?

GREG

I just saw him move.

CLAIR

That's impossible, –

JILL

He's unconscious.

CLAIR

(JOHN starts to move some more) Oh my goodness. *(Runs over to JOHN)* Aaron, can you hear me?

JOHN

Mom…

ALEX

(Runs over to CLAIR) Aaron, son, how are you feeling?

JOHN

Dad, is that you?

CLAIR

Yes, it's your mom and dad.

JOHN

(He slowly opens his eyes). Mom, where am I?

CLAIR

You're in the hospital. You were unconscious, but you're going to be okay.

JILL

(Sings) I'm going to need you guys to leave.

JOHN

(Everyone one on stage is confused, and frustrated, except John, whom enjoys JILL's costume) No mommy, don't leave.

CLAIR

(Looking at Jill angrily) Its okay Aaron, we'll be here, we'll be right outside the door.*(blackout)*

MARIA

(Lights comes up by audience. It is intermission the audience exits the theater.) What the hell was that?

BRIAN

It was pretty good. Jill has a great voice, and she can dance too.

MARIA

I'm going to kill her. *(Frustrated)* That was garbage, all of it. What are they trying to do to me? (Pause)I hope you plan on going backstage now. Don't forget you are operating the light board.

BRIAN

Well, I figured, since it is the last scene, I'll leave the scene before and go backstage.

MARIA

No, that'll be too late. Brian, why can't you go backstage now?

BRIAN

Because, I'm enjoying the show. I don't remember this being rehearsed.

MARIA

(The audience has returned by now). That's because it wasn't. I don't believe this. Brian, please go backstage. So much bad things have happened already. I don't need anything else going wrong.

BRIAN

Why not, what's one more bad thing?

MARIA

Brian, go backstage.

BRIAN

I'll go after the first scene. I promise.

MARIA

(The lights dim to a black out. Act two begins. As the lights dim the audience applause). Brian, would you please–

BRIAN

Shh! It's about to start.

CLAIR

(JOHN enters and lies on the bed. CLAIR sits on chair next to him, a brief black out occurs then the lights slowly fade in). Remember when I used to read to you at night, before you went to bed? *(JOHN nods head yes. CLAIR shows JOHN a book).* You mind if I read to you?

JOHN

I would love that. It'll bring back sweet memories.

CLAIR

(Opens children's book), and reads. As she reads GREG enters. As she is reading JOHN looks up at GREG, after glancing at JOHN she turns around and sees GREG, GREG becomes frightened). Not you again, get out, and don't come back.

JOHN

(GREG intends to leave) No, don't leave. Mom, I want to talk to him *(There is another camera flash seen).*

CLAIR

Aaron, he is bad news. I don't want you around people like him.

JOHN

Mom, please I must speak with him. *(CLAIR shakes her head yes as a hesitant approval; she exits. GREG sits down next to JOHN. There is complete silence for about 5 seconds. After the pause they both recite each other's name).* I'm sorry you go first.

GREG

No, no, you; tell me what you need to tell me.

JOHN

Jason, please you go first, I can wait. *(GREG folds his arms as if in protest to speak first).* Alright, I'll go first. I'm sorry I ruined your party.

GREG

Are you crazy? You didn't ruin it. I'm sorry I gave you all that stuff. I didn't know it was going to make you…I'm sorry.

JOHN

Come up here. *(As GREG sits on the bed, it collapses and John and Greg fall through it. John tries to continue the scene. Brian is laughing loud).* I know you think this is your fault *(trying to get up)* my mom thinks it's her fault. This is no one's fault but, mine. *(Still trying to get up; Greg is trying to get up and help John)* I made the decision to take ecstasy and drink beer. I was the one who did not use discretion. It is my fault. So, please, stop blaming yourself, *(brief silence, and blackout).*

SARAH

(When the lights come up SARAH and the party extras are on stage, they party for a brief moment before GREG enters, SARAH notices him). Hey stranger, long time no see. Where have you been?

GREG

I went to visit Aaron.

SARAH

How's the slugger doing?

GREG

He's doing. *(Beat)* Uh…Lizzie I need to talk to you alone.

SARAH

Jason, we're partying, party with us. We can talk later.

GREG

No. I want to talk now. *(GREG talks to the party extras).* Excuse me; may I have your attention? *(The party and music stop).* The party is over; everyone please leave. *(The party people adlib disapproval)* Come on, get out. *(They begin to leave).*

CLAIR

(Off stage) AHHHH!! Get it away from me.

SARAH

(Acting like she didn't hear anything; pulling him aside) What is wrong with you? You're ruining a good thing. *(Talking to the party people)* Guys, you don't have to leave.

JOHN

(Offstage) What's wrong; why are you screaming?

CLAIR

(Offstage) I just saw a mouse.

JOHN

(Offstage) I thought Brian took care of that problem *(a mouse trap snaps, JOHN screams)* THAT HURT!!

JILL

(Offstage) What's going on *(snap)* AHHHH!! What the hell was that

JOHN

(Offstage) A mouse trap.

JILL

(Offstage) Why are there mouse traps back here *(snap)* Ohhh!

JOHN

(Offstage) Because there are mice back here *(snap)* Ohhh!

JILL

(Offstage) How many are back here?

JOHN

(Offstage) I don't know *(snap)* Ohh!

CLAIR

(Offstage) Don't be so loud. They can probably here you out there.

JOHN

(Offstage) Shut up Clair, *(snap)* AHHH!

GREG

(Everyone on stage is trying to ignore the backstage interruptions) Yes you do. Everyone out *(beat)* now.

SARAH

(Party extras exit). What is wrong with you? You never turn down a party.

GREG

I'm changing, Lizzie…I've changed. I can't do this anymore.

SARAH

You can't do what anymore; what are you talking about?

GREG

I can't live this lifestyle. No more parties, drugs, alcohol, it ruins lives. It makes people unconscious and—

JOHN

(Offstage; snap) Ohh!

SARAH

Are you still worried about Aaron? Get over it. Aaron is fine. Besides, he was a punk; he took too much too soon. You're a pro; you can keep partying without passing out.

GREG

Lizzie, I do not want to do this anymore. I am done with it, and you should be done with it too.

SARAH

What the hell is going on with you? If you won't party anymore, I'm afraid our friendship is over.

GREG

That is not a problem with me; you know where the door is. *(SARAH exits, blackout).*

MARIA

(The set is being changed; once it is finished; GREG, SARAH, JILL, and, EXTRAS enter. At this point there is still a black out.) Why is there still a blackout? What is wrong with Brian?

BRIAN

What did you say?

MARIA

Who said that?

BRIAN

Me, Brian.

MARIA

(Frustrated) You're supposed to be backstage managing the lights

BRIAN

Oh no, did I forget?

MARIA

BRIAN.

BRIAN

I'm going. *(Brian runs on stage bumps into some people, apologizes, then exits to backstage)*

JOHN

(Lights come up. There is music playing softly in the background. ALEX, CLAIR and JOHN enter. When they enter, the lights come up and everyone on stage yells "Surprise!"). Oh, my goodness, this is wonderful. *(We can see his pain; he hugs ALEX and then CLAIR)* THANKS dad, thanks mom, you have made me so happy. I want to thank all of you for coming. Most of all I want to thank you all for the love and support you showed me while I was in the hospital. I made some stupid choices and I had to pay the consequences. I just thank God that I'm still alive. Thanks again. *(Everyone cheers, and returns to partying (drinking, dancing, conversing)).*

UNCLE JACOB

(Clair and Alex walk toward the guest to thank and welcome them. UNCLE JACOB and AUNT GLORIA walk towards JOHN. JACOB gives JOHN a rough hug) Hey, there's my nephew.

JOHN

Uncle Jake.

UNCLE JACOB

How are you doing, buddy, you keeping out of trouble?

JOHN

Yes, I am doing the best that I can.

AUNT GLORIA

(Hugs JOHN) How are you Aaron, you feeling well *(JOHN nods yes)*? That's good.

UNCLE JACOB

(Tries to wrestle with JOHN) Of course, he's okay. He's my slugger.

AUNT GLORIA

Jake, calm down.

UNCLE JACOB

Gloria, don't tell me what to do.

AUNT GLORIA

Well, if you weren't acting like a child I wouldn't have to.

UNCLE JACOB

What is your problem?

AUNT GLORIA

There is nothing wrong with me, however, your problem is too much beer. *(Beat)* Slow down before you hurt yourself. *(UNCLE JACOB and AUNT GLORIA walk away arguing).*

USHER

(Another camera flash is seen. USHER walks towards WOMAN) Excuse ma'am, I'm afraid I'm going to have to take your camera.

WOMAN

You can't do that, *(beat)* it's mine.

USHER

Yes it is, but you've been warned, woman. I'm going to have to take it.

WOMAN

No, I won't let you. *(The WOMAN and USHER fight over the camera, finally the usher grabs the camera)* Give me the camera *(he throws it and it lands on the stage; the USHER returns to his position).*

JOHN

(GREG walks towards JOHN. JOHN sees him and smiles. He puts his hand towards GREG and they shake hands). Hey, thanks for coming.

GREG

When your mom called me I thought she was plotting my death *(They both laugh).*

JOHN

She was upset; after I talked to her she realize you weren't all that bad. *(Changing the subject)* So, how's Lizzie and the rest of the crew.

GREG

I don't know, *(beat)* I don't hang out with them anymore. I changed, after I saw you in the hospital I had to stop.

JOHN

That's good. I'm happy for you.

GREG

I'm happy for you too. To see you alive is a good feeling. *(Pause)* I'm sorry—

JOHN

Don't apologize; *(pause)* it's good seeing you again *(he puts his hands toward Greg and they shake, then they hug.*

CLAIR

(CLAIR and JILL walk towards JOHN). Aaron, look who is here.

JOHN

(He looks and smiles, he walks to JILL and hugs her) Grandma Rose thanks for coming. You didn't have to travel so far for me.

JILL

I know, but you're worth it. How are you puff cakes?

JOHN

I'm doing much better, now that I know you're here.

JILL

Ain't he sweet *(takes a dollar out of her purse)* here you go puff cakes, don't spend it all on one place. *(Walking away with CLAIR and speaking to her)* What do you have to drink?

CLAIR

We have juice, water, soda—

JILL

Do you have any liquor?

JOHN

(Talking to GREG, referring to dollar) This may not look like a lot, but the last time I saw her she gave me fifty cents *(They laugh)*.

GREG

That's funny. *(Beat)* Explain something for me.

JOHN

What?

GREG

Puff cakes?

JOHN

(Laughing) When I was a baby, I had big puffy cheeks *(beat)* she's been calling me that ever since then.

ALEX

(Banging fork against glass, to get everyone's attention) May I have everyone's attention? I want to make a toast to the best son a father could have. *(Everyone has a drink already, Jill brings a glass to Aaron, and Clair brings one to Greg).* Although he made his mistakes, he still is a son that makes me very proud. If I had a choice, I wouldn't want any other young gentleman as my son. He's the best son ever, *(he raises his glass)* cheers *(Everyone cheers and toast each other and drink. The background music gets louder and everyone dances, the light goes out slowly. When the lights come up the actors do curtain calls; after curtain calls a black out occurs and the actors exit the stage; the lights come up).*

MARIA

(The audience members stand and talk amongst themselves.) I am going back there and killing each and every one of them. *(The light goes out and a light comes up on the backstage area. Maria enters).* I want to see everyone's face out here, right now! *(Everyone enters).* What the hell was that? That's not what we rehearsed. Jill, I should kill you. How dare you pull a stunt like that. John, Sarah, and Jill, the mouse hunters, do you think you could have been louder. Brian, that's why I said to stay backstage. What were you doing? Your work was terrible tonight.

BILLY

Well, we still have nine more shows to do it better.

MARIA

(Angry) We might not have another try,' cause chances are this show is being closed.

BRIAN

Everything wasn't our fault. I told you the bed wasn't strong enough for the both of them. You said the bed was fine, so, that part is your fault. And also, the chairs, I said the chairs–

MARIA

You're not allowed to speak to me.

ANTHONY

(Enters) Hey Maria.

MARIA

Anthony, hi. Oh, my gosh. You have to excuse that mess you saw. Wait a minute. How did you get back here?

ANTHONY

Don't worry about that. Guess who was sitting in the audience and wants to speak with you?

MARIA

I don't know. I really don't wanna play guessing games at this moment.

ANTHONY

Viola Stephanie.

MARIA

What?! You can't be serious?

BRIAN

Who's Viola Stephanie

MARIA

She's the playwright *(she looks at JILL with anger; JILL puts her head down)*.

BRIAN

What's a playwright

CLAIR

Someone who writes plays.

BRIAN

What play did she write, maybe we should do one of her plays next year.

MARIA

You idiot, we did one of her plays this year.

BRIAN

Oh, *(pauses, realizes who VIOLA is)* Oh, so this isn't good, right?

MARIA

Jill, I did not know she was coming to see this. What do I tell her?

JILL

(Nervous) I don't know. I'm sorry, I didn't know. I was just trying to get noticed by Anthony.

ANTHONY

You did a good job.

JILL

Oh really, thank you, I was trying to– *(Maria gives her an angry look, she stops talking).*

MARIA

I don't believe this *(beat)* my career is over.

ANTHONY

Are you ready to meet her?

MARIA

(Looks at everyone) Pray for me *(Blackout)*.

ACT TWO SCENE THREE

MARIA

The lights come up on the auditorium. The audience members are ad-libbing in the background. Maria enters. She is afraid to face Viola. She walks towards her.) Wow, Viola *(puts her hand out and they shake)* What a pleasure to meet you. Before you say anything let me explain. This is not what we rehearsed for two months; I promise. I have no clue what happened tonight. I just want to–

VIOLA

This was the most awful drama I have ever seen.

MARIA

I am so sorry I ruined your play.

VIOLA

What were you thinking?

MARIA

This is not how it was supposed to go. Everything went wrong.

VIOLA

Did you know this was suppose to be a drama.

MARIA

I know, I didn't mean to–

VIOLA

It was the funniest thing I have ever seen. I enjoyed it so much.

MARIA

Please, let me explain, I didn't mean to– what did you say?

VIOLA

You have changed my play.

MARIA

I didn't do it on purpose, honest.

VIOLA

Well, I think you have made a good mistake. You have made a great comedy from a drama. You know, most directors can't do that.

MARIA

Well, I wasn't trying to–

VIOLA

This is great. We gotta take this on the road. We have to adapt the play, and give it a new name. All my life I have been trying to have a successful comedy.

MARIA

You have?

VIOLA

Yes, but it never happened. People enjoyed my dramas better than my comedies. And then you come along and make the people enjoy a Viola comedy.

MARIA

Are you serious?

VIOLA

Yes. This is amazing. You know what. We are going to work together.

MARIA

What? Me work with you? It would be an honor.

VIOLA

We can turn all my drama into comedies. We can start with... um... with... oh *The Sadness of Funerals*.

MARIA

That's one of your best dramas. You can't tun that into a comedy. It involves people dying.

VIOLA

Until today, I wouldn't have believe it either. But you showed me anything can be done. Maria I want you to get your troupe–

MARIA

My troupe?

VIOLA

Yes, your actors, your crew members, your company...your...your posse, what ever the hell you wanna call it, and we are going to make history together.

MARIA

You have to be joking.

VIOLA

No, I'm not joking *(hands her a business card)* give me a call. *(Starts to cry)* You have made me proud.

MARIA

(Looks at card) It'll be my pleasure. It was nice meeting you *(Maria intends to shake Viola's hand, instead Viola grabs and hugs her, then she exits. Maria is looking at the card)* oh my gosh, I don't believe this. *(As she is amazed Anthony approaches her).*

ANTHONY

Hey, how are you?

MARIA

Anthony, I want to apologize for that...mess. I don't know what happened.

ANTHONY

No, it was pretty good. It was really funny.

MARIA

But it wasn't supposed to be. Please don't write a review. My life will be over if you do so.

ANTHONY

Why not?!

MARIA

If word get's around of how bad it was, no one will come and see it. And then I won't have money for the fund-raiser.

ANTHONY

Don't worry, it was a blast. No one liked this play until now. You have made a terrible script into a terrific production. I want to write a review.

MARIA

Please don't do that. I feel like a failure.

ANTHONY

Why? I over heard your conversation with Viola. Seems like she enjoyed it. What's the problem?

MARIA

The problem is, I set out to make everyone like this play because of it's drama. It spoke to me, to my soul. I cried when I read this. I wanted people to leave here in tears.

ANTHONY

(Laughing, wiping tears) Well, some of us did.

MARIA

I mean tears of sadness.

ANTHONY

It doesn't matter. The most important thing is that they enjoyed it. They'll go home and tell all their family and friends to come see it. If enough word gets around this place will be packed. Then you'll have more than enough for the fund-raiser, and that's what's more important, right?

MARIA

Yeah, I guess you're right. It's just weird how things happen.

ANTHONY

Yeah, that's life. *(Beat)* How would you like it if I treated you to a celebration dinner.

MARIA

You don't have to do that.

ANTHONY

I know, but I want to. Please, it would give me pleasure to get to know you better *(he takes her hand and kisses it)*.

MARIA

(Blushing) Well, you sure know how to treat a lady. *(He takes her hand and they begin to exit)* So, Mr Bridges, tell me about yourself.

ANTHONY

Well, I'm single; *(beat)* hopefully that'll change in a couple of hours.

MARIA

It already has.

CURTAINS

ALTERNATE ENDING ACT TWO SCENE THREE
ACT TWO SCENE THREE

MARIA

The lights come up on the auditorium. The audience members are ad-libbing in the background. Maria enters. She is afraid to face Viola. She walks towards her.) Wow, Viola *(puts her hand out and they shake)* What a pleasure to meet you. Before you say anything let me explain. This is not what we rehearsed for two months; I promise. I have no clue what happened tonight. I just want to–

VIOLA

This is the worst opening night I ever witnessed.

MARIA

I am so sorry. Please forgive me. We had a great dress rehearsal last night; I don't know what happened.

VIOLA

I'm just so speechless.

MARIA

I know I shouldn't ask you this, but would you mind coming back tomorrow. I know for sure it will be better. What you saw tonight is not our best.

VIOLA

I would hope not. It doesn't even look like you guys were ready to open.

MARIA

I know, I know, but, please, understand that tonight was just a mistake. Someone must have said Macbeth or something, I don't know. All I know is I want you to see the version we did last night and I know we can do a better job. It must have been opening night jitters.

VIOLA

Well, I am in town for the weekend. I guess I can swing by here tomorrow night.

MARIA

Oh please do, I promise it will be much, *much* better.

VIOLA

Okay. I'm taking your word.

MARIA

I promise. Thank you so much.

VIOLA

No problem. Now, you go get some rest. I think you need it. *(Viola exits.)*

MARIA

Okay, I will. Thank you again. It was nice meeting you *(Anthony approaches her)*.

ANTHONY

Hey, how are you?

MARIA

Anthony, I want to apologize for that...mess. I don't know what happened.

ANTHONY

No, it was pretty good. It was really funny.

MARIA

But it wasn't supposed to be funny. Please don't write a review.

ANTHONY

Don't worry. I'll be back tomorrow night along with Ms. Viola.

MARIA

Oh goodness. You heard that?

ANTHONY

Yeah. Don't worry. At least she understands.

MARIA

I feel like a failure.

ANTHONY

Don't feel that way. *(Beat)* How would you like it if I treated you to dinner?

MARIA

You don't have to do that.

ANTHONY

I know, but I want to. Please, it would give me pleasure to get to know you better *(he takes her hand and kisses it)*.

JILL'S SONG

When people look at me they think I'm a nurse.

Some even think I'm a front desk clerk

But I assure you, I'm not a nurse

I'm not even a plain ole doctor

I am Ms. Doctor Love

Come and get your healing

Ms. Doctor Love

I'm more than appealing

I can rub your back

And what you lack I can give you

I'm Ms. doctor love

A gift from up above

Ms. Doctor Love

The one you're dreaming of

For I am Ms. Doctor Love

Dance Break

They say to eat an apple a day

To keep me away

And drink three glasses of milk to keep you fine as silk

But if it's milk you want

Its milk I've got

So, don't you run away

'Cause I'll be your apple a day

For I am Ms. Doctor Love

I know what you're feeling

Ms. Doctor Love

Come and get your healing

Ms. Doctor Love

I'm much more than appealing

For I am Ms. Doctor Love

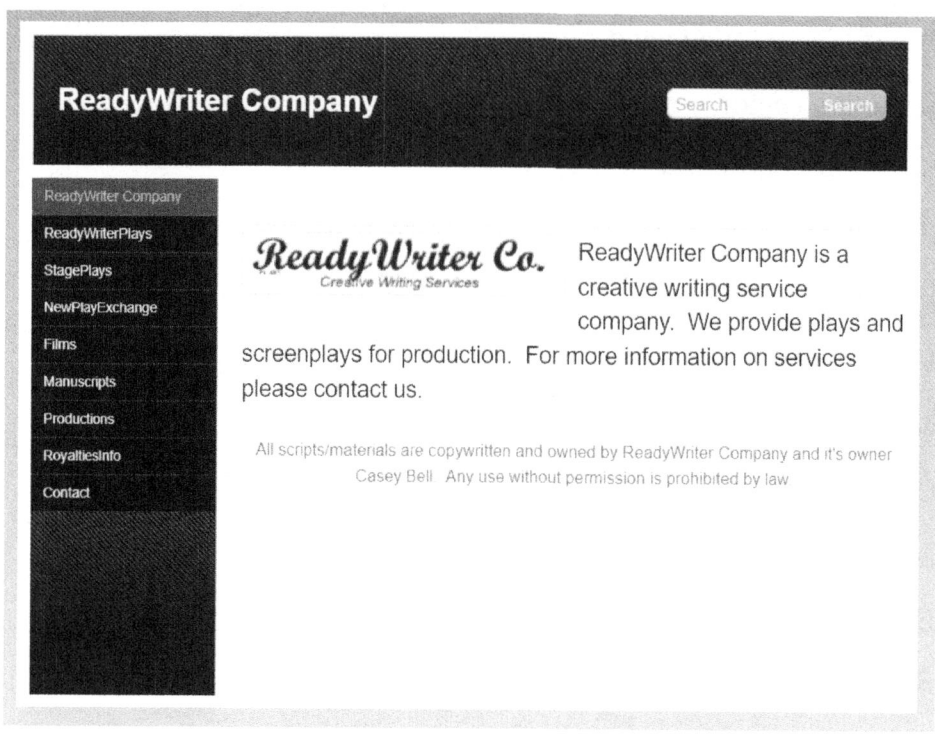

readywritercsb.com

Made in the USA
Monee, IL
27 June 2023

37810614R00118